SPANISH MOSS

FURTHER

BRONZEVILLE
— BOOKS —

Bronzeville Books Inc.
269 S. Beverly Drive, #202
Beverly Hills, CA 90212
www.bronzevillebooks.com

Library of Congress Control Number: 2020948920

ISBN - 978-1-952427-11-4

10 9 8 7 6 5 4 3 2 1

SPANISH MOSS

EDDY COOK

For Dave Mullin.
You know.

1

CALVIN SPENT LONG periods of time alone. His mother, he was told, had long since left with another man. His father, Thomas Gasparilla, was a mean drunk who kept Calvin and his much older sister Theresa constantly on the move in an RV held together with rust and bondo. Odd jobs kept the three of them in hamburger helper and government cheese.

Because his sister was fourteen years older than him, Calvin had no one to have adventures with, they never parked in RV parks, and he never had a chance to make friends. Although Theresa was very protective of him, taking blows from their abusive father while trying to grab the big man's arms to protect the boy, she spent most of the time keeping things clean, cooking and home-schooling Calvin. As a result, she had very little time to have fun with Calvin.

The family had been camped by a lake in Minnesota when, while their father was MIA on the evening of Calvin's fifteenth birthday, Theresa sat him down and told him the family's darkest secret; that she was in fact his sister, and his mother. Her mother had escaped years ago, and Theresa had become their father's new toy and that was why she slept in the back room with him. Along with this revelation came a warning; Dad liked boys too. Teen boys. Theresa told Calvin that she had been carefully sneaking small amounts of money from their dad's wallet when he was sleeping and was waiting until she had enough for at least Calvin to get away but until that day, she said she wanted him to be careful not to be alone with their father.

A year later, camped near another lake in Minnesota just after Calvin turned sixteen, his father came to him at night where the boy slept, toward the front of the RV on the kitchen table that converted to a bed. Since his conversation with Theresa, Calvin had kept a kitchen knife under his pillow. On the night that his father threw the covers back and tried to climb on top of him, Calvin stabbed him in the heart. The big man growled through his teeth and rolled off him and landed on the floor, clutching for the knife in his chest. The traumatized boy watched as the life left the open eyes of his father seconds later.

Calvin got up quickly and began shaking all over, his legs weak and wobbling as Theresa came running to him and saw what had happened.

"I have to leave now," Calvin said quietly, his voice trembling.

"No, I'll figure out a way to take care of us," Theresa said, as they both looked down at their dead abuser.

Calvin shook his head and, more calmly, said, "I want to. I want to see and touch everything. All the people, places and things that you taught me about, I really want to be free and I want you to get a chance to live, not always taking care of things, or me. You're like, thirty years old. You deserve a life. It's our turn to live."

Theresa looked hard into his eyes, saw the firm set of his jaw. Neither of them spoke as they backed away from the room, instinctively putting space between them and the corpse.

They both found a place to sit and Theresa bent over, head in her hands, and said nothing for a full minute as Calvin looked out the window, staring absently at nothing, lost in his own thoughts.

When Theresa looked up and saw the young man's jaw was still set, she nodded and said, "Okay."

She quickly packed a small backpack with clothes and snacks for him and handed him $140 that she had and another fifty that she dug out of their dead father's wallet.

"You're almost grown and you're smart. I'll take care of this. Go back up this dirt road to the highway and start hitchhiking. I love you."

He knew she was right and took off at a trot toward the unknown, sobbing.

They were camped illegally near a lake and no-one was around as she wrapped the big man's body in a blanket, pulled as hard as she could until she bounced him down the two steps to the ground and struggled with all her might to drag his body to the shore where she pulled the floating body into chest-high water and left it floating there for a moment as she waded back to shore, grabbed a large rock, waded out to set it on the corpse's chest and watched as the dead monster sank.

ONLY SEVENTEEN AND already Calvin was weary. Living on the road and the streets he learned in a few short days how to read people and stay alive, but he had been on the move for seven months and he was worn out.

Headlights coming around the curve of the I-10 causeway in Louisiana gave him a spark of hope. It was 2 a.m., and it had been so long since he had seen a car. Fifty feet below was the bayou; predators making their night noises had kept him on edge.

Adjusting his duffle, he rose from the guardrail and faced the car as it approached. Calvin raised his thumb high, worried that the six feet between the guard-rail and the white line weren't enough for the car to pull over.

When the driver was within fifty yards he suddenly swerved a little, threw on his high-beams, and began to slow down. Passing Calvin, he pulled over to the shoulder, leaving just enough room between the car and the guardrail to pop open the passenger-side door. Relieved, Calvin trotted up to the maroon Cadillac and peered inside.

"Get in, boy," the driver growled.

"Watch the paint job and throw your stuff in the back seat."

Seven months on the road had given Calvin a well-honed "freak radar." Every hair on his neck prickled as he paused, looking into the small, pig-like eyes of the well dressed, overweight driver. The boy's fatigue and a greater fear of the faceless noises waiting in the bayou below were enough to cause him to ignore instinct. Opening the back door, he tossed his duffle on the white leather seat and settled into the front passenger seat.

"Damn, boy! Thought you'd never get in," the moon-faced driver said.

In the instant before the dome-light went out, Calvin saw him lick his lips and grin. As the driver merged back onto the deserted highway, Calvin's senses were assaulted by cigar smoke, Zydeco music playing too loud from the car stereo, and finally by the Polaroid photos taped to the dash directly over the steering wheel. He had missed them when he first got in, and now the rage built up in him, the pictures, partially lit by the instrument panel, were of different boys between the ages of ten and maybe fifteen. Some were naked, some in underwear, all of them in suggestive poses.

"Hey boy, I see you lookin', you like my art gallery?" Pig-Eyes said.

He reached over, put a hand on Calvin's knee and gave it a squeeze.

"No!" Calvin hissed through gritted teeth as he sent a palm heel into the driver's nose at an upward angle. The impact pushed all the bones of the driver's nasal cavity into his brain. He was dead before the Caddy's front bumper crashed through the guardrail at 70 mph.

Calvin had barely enough time to scream and curl into a ball under the dashboard before the maroon car went airborne, and within seconds crashed hood first into the thicket of cypress trees sticking out of the murky bayou below.

On impact with the tree tops the car rolled sharply to the left and plunged driver's side first into the slime-covered, green-black depths of the bayou.

When the Caddy had come to rest, Calvin found himself sitting on the corpse of the driver, which was under two feet of swamp water. He stood on the body and was repulsed at the squishy feel below his shoes as he quickly reached above his head, opened the passenger-side window and pulled himself up to what was now the top of the car.

He scrabbled across the upturned side of the car, opened the back door, and pulled his half-submerged duffel from the back seat.

Trembling from shock, he sat on a door and assessed his injuries. Gingerly moving his limbs, he determined nothing was broken, but everything hurt. Feeling sticky wetness on his face, he drew a couple fingers through the moisture. In the moonlit Louisiana night his fingers appeared black, but the wetness was warm and he knew he was bleeding steadily from his temple. Calvin reached in his duffel, found a pair of dry socks near the top, and tied them together at the openings. Putting the knot behind his head, he drew the one side around what felt to be a two inch laceration, and tied the toe-ends together at his fore-head.

Around him the bayou spoke in whispering hisses, twigs snapping, splashes and bubbling both far off and far too near. The car below him sank slowly. Muddy, sucking noises told Calvin that his metal island was soon to become a submerged snack container for the gators that surely lurked nearby.

Standing, he carefully swung his duffle over a branch of the nearest of the trees he had crashed through minutes before and clipped one of the shoulder-straps around the limb. With his hands gripping another stronger limb higher up, Calvin lifted both feet high, hooked his heels, and shimmied his way to the trunk. Finding more hand holds, he swung around until he sat securely in a V where the tree split naturally.

From his position, no plan seemed feasible. Judging by the slowly sinking Caddy, the mud bottom below the surface of the swamp was like quicksand. Swimming with his duffle in tow, in the moonlit dark of the bayou, with few gnarly swamp trees spread far from each other, seemed like an unlikely option. He heard something large slip into the water from its hiding place.

2

CALVIN'S EYES GREW heavy as the shock wore off. He sat watching as the water level rose above the side of the car and the maroon tomb sank out of sight. A bright light shone out of the darkness directly over the last swirling ripples.

Alert now, Calvin turned carefully from his roost to find the source of the sudden light in the darkness. The floodlight seemed to float toward him on its own. Blinded, he couldn't see beyond it as it rose to expose his position.

From behind the light a man's voice, barely audible, came across the swamp.

"Your car flies, but it does not swim so well," the stranger said, as his shallow, flat-bottomed boat came into focus through the fading spots in Calvin's eyes.

"It's not my car." Calvin's response came out almost a whisper.

In an accent Calvin had never heard before the man said, "Will you stay in the tree, or climb down and get in the pirogue?"

"Pee-row?" His heart quickened, this man before him seemed too good to be true. "You mean the boat?"

"Oui, the boat. Hand me your bag first, e'r so carefully, and come down." The quiet baritone of the man's voice, and the calm demeanor of the weather-worn face as it came into view directly under the tree, was assurance enough. Calvin shifted his weight, grabbed the duffel by the strap, and lowered it as instructed.

The man stood slowly, feet spread wide for stability, and grabbed the bag, placing it directly in the middle of the odd-looking craft, and sat back down.

Calvin swung down, his feet only a few inches from the bottom of the boat.

"Ver' carefully now, when you let go, bend your knees."

Calvin landed in a crouch, barely rocking the craft, and immediately sat down opposite his rescuer.

The soft-spoken man turned off the light mounted on the side of the craft, reached under his seat, brought out a battery powered lantern, turned it on and placed it on the deck between his knee-high rubber boots.

"My name is Esteen." The man's voice was altogether quiet, strong, and calming.

"Mine's Calvin."

"The driver of the car, he was bad. No?"

"Yes, Sir."

After a pause, Esteen grabbed something from the seat beside him. Calvin recognized it as one of the Polaroids from the dashboard.

"I grab this from the water when I drifted up. One look tells me enough, I think. No loss, this driver."

"No, Sir." Calvin said, waiting.

"We go to my place. Change the dressing on your head, okay?" Esteen's Cajun accent was, Calvin knew from TV, not quite French and very fascinating.

"Yes, Sir. Thank you."

Esteen grabbed an eight-foot pole from the floor of the pirogue and pushed off from the crash site. By moonlight alone he navigated the obstacles in the bayou with confidence. Neither he nor Calvin looked back.

After a few minutes on an easterly course, Esteen banked to the south a few yards, stopped near a floating plastic bottle and laid the pole in the boat. Shining his floodlight in the water he reached below the surface, grabbed the thin rope that the bottle was tethered to, and pulled up a cylindrical cage teeming with crawfish. Shaking it well to rid it of water, he laid it in the craft near Calvin's duffel. Without a word, he picked up the pole and continued east.

At one point as they drifted, Calvin saw the eye-shine of a gator swimming parallel to the pirogue for a few yards. In a minute, the eyes submerged.

Safe. Maybe. Calvin could not remember ever feeling safe. But for now, in this place and time, he did. Never had he met a man whose presence demanded his respect. Calvin had no meter of what a man should be, he learned what he knew from the few books he had read and the many movies he had watched. Not from the human called his father. The man before him, quietly and confidently guiding him through the Louisiana night, had thus far asked nothing in return.

Calvin shook his head, feeling the pain of his injury, and reminding himself not to get too comfortable. Life was hard. People were not what they seemed. No-one could be trusted. These truths kept him one step ahead. Kept him alive.

They had been afloat for twenty minutes when a small cabin came into view. By the moonlight Calvin could make out the peculiar stilts that held the building three feet above the water. Looking around, he could see no solid land. No bridge leading to the home. Nothing he had seen on the T.V. or read in books had prepared him for the sight before him. It was so . . . solitary.

A faint, flickering light shone in the window facing them as Esteen tied the front of the craft to a short dock. No words were spoken between them as they climbed up onto the dock and emptied the pirogue of crawfish and gear. The boy watched as Esteen busied himself on the dock, rinsing the crawfish and filling a drum with fresh water from a hand pump. He added salt and lit a fire under the drum to boil the catch.

Turning as one, they headed toward the door, each with their own load to carry, when the door was pushed open from the inside.

3

AS THE CABIN door opened wider, an old woman rolled out onto the dock in an antique wheelchair with high wheels. Intricately patterned cloth covered the arm rests and ornate metal push-handles, each with the image of a water moccasin coiled around an alligator etched deeply into the metal.

As she turned toward them, the kerosene lamplight that emanated from the cabin highlighted her features. She was beyond ancient. Deep and fine lines accented her features, her skin paper thin and deeply tanned. At first glance, Calvin saw an unnatural light emanating from her stunning azurite eyes.

He was speechless and stood in place and stared.

"This is my mama, you may call her Miss Jovetta," Esteen said, pronouncing 'this' so it sounded like 'thees.'

"So sorry, I've forgotten your name, mon ami," he said, looking at Calvin.

To Miss Jovetta, Calvin said, "It's Calvin, Ma'am."

"Such a polite boy. You must come from fine stock."

"No, Ma'am. I do not."

"Ah, so you've chosen to be well mannered, oui?"

"Yes, Ma'am," he said.

Her voice seemed to be that of a woman of forty, rather than the ninety or more years she must have behind her. A beautiful voice with the same calming effect as Esteen's.

"Your aura is fiercely orange, but at the edges it is dark," she said.

"You understand the meaning of aura? It is something that only I see. Like a light around you. It tells me you are so damaged and alone, I think." "Come into the kitchen and I will put some Spanish moss on your injury. Come child and rest."

Miss Jovetta offered Calvin a seat at the modest, handmade dining table which sat under the cabin's only window. "You call me Miss Jovetta, ok?" "Yes Ma ..." he began to say, then quickly corrected himself, "Miss Jovetta."

"I am pleased to have you in my home," she said.

Calvin thought a moment and said, "I don't think anyone has been pleased to have me in their home before." Not fishing for sympathy. Only speaking the truth.

Gliding next to him in her masterpiece antique chair, Miss Jovetta tenderly reached for the dressing on the young man's head. Unused to a kind touch, he flinched, and his eyes grew wide. She gently reached up again, this time looking into his eyes and smiling. Gingerly, she continued to remove the makeshift headband. Her gnarled fingers were surprisingly deft.

From a wicker box on the table she removed a small bit of Spanish moss wrapped in a large leaf. Setting the moss in a bowl, she poured water on it and let it soak. The mysterious, gentle elder removed a cloth from a fold in her gingham dress, dipped it in the water, and wiped the dried blood around the laceration.

Much as Calvin's sister looked out for him, she rarely offered a loving touch. The tender touch of this stranger brought tears to his eyes, and he could feel burning in his cheeks.

As the old woman continued to tend to him, securing the moss to his wound, tears ran hot down his cheeks in streams and he let out a long shaky sigh. Calvin didn't resist as she pulled him into her bosom, and he fell asleep listening as she hummed a soothing tune.

4

MISS JOVETTA SHOOK his foot gently and Calvin woke up on a fold-out cot that Esteen had provided the night before. When he saw that it was her who woke him, he smiled. When he sat up, she said, "We use this cabin when we catch crawfish and sometimes gators, but we will be going home soon. Do you know how to paddle a canoe?"

"Yes ma'am. I've lived near lakes and have been canoeing. I got pretty good, I guess." As Calvin said this, his stomach growled audibly.

At this, the woman chuckled, winked, and said, "Oui, I hear your belly. Sit by the table and I'll fill you with shrimp gumbo, and corn bread."

Without hesitation, the young man made his way to a chair. As the elder hostess went about getting his meal, Esteen pointed to the rafters of the cabin and said, "The canoe up there, do you see? We will have you follow us in that."

Calvin only nodded as he filled his mouth with the cornbread on the plate that was put before him. As he ate, he looked at the canoe. He had not noticed it before, and now marveled at its craftsmanship. It was made of a rich, bronze wood. The craft seemed to have been made from a single log, smooth and sturdy. At the bow was carved the same symbol he had noticed on the handles of the wheelchair; a snake coiled around an alligator.

Esteen set about filling an army rucksack with food and other supplies. From a tray on her lap, Miss Jovetta set a bowl of gumbo, a spoon, and a glass of lemonade in front of Calvin. Wordlessly he attacked the gumbo, which drew a spectacular smile from the mysterious, ancient woman.

Again, the young man was taken aback by the deep beauty of a woman so old. Her gleaming azurite eyes, and unlikely white teeth, added to her mystique.

Esteen pulled the canoe down carefully, easing it backwards out the door and out of sight.

"We will go far from here," Miss Jovetta said. "To a place that has been in our family for nigh onto two hundred years."

5

WATCHING INTENTLY AS Esteen gently lifted his mother from her chair, lightly seating her in the rear of the pirogue, Calvin could not recall seeing love and respect between family members. He offered to load the antique chair into his canoe, but the older man explained that it wouldn't be needed, and that out on the bayou things stayed where you left them. Stealing was almost unheard of.

The young man's education had already begun. New rules were being established. Only one day ago, life was survival. Period. Black and gray were the colors. Calvin's own heartbeat had been the only rhythm. Things were looking up.

With both his duffel and the rucksack loaded, Calvin stepped into his craft, released the paddles from their leather straps and, on command, began long slow strokes as he followed the boat before him.

The setting sun served as a compass as they drifted west. The swamp gave up a pungent aroma as both crafts stirred the thin film of the bayou surface. Hummingbirds could be seen flittering low, snatching bugs in their paths. Off to one side, a turtle tracked the boats from its perch on a drifting log. The small wake was enough to send it sliding into the water.

An hour passed, pirogue and canoe making a long S shaped westward path, when Miss Jovetta turned and told Calvin that inside his duffel was a snack. The momentum of his last strokes propelled him as he paused long enough to extract some jerked meat strips from his gear.

He ate these and paddled on as sunset became twilight, and twilight became night.

Behind them the moon came on duty, and it was by this soft light they traveled. Hummingbirds and turtles found their resting places and turned the Louisiana night over to the carnivores, snakes, and other nocturnal wanderers that made stealthy, almost imperceptible noises.

Three hours of traveling brought the trio to dry land. As they approached the shore, Esteen stepped out of the pirogue and drug it to a sandbar which was at the base of a hill. Motioning for Calvin to pull up beside them, Esteen grabbed the bow of the canoe and pulled it in. The quiet man leaned into his craft, cradled his mother in his arms, and carried her to what appeared to Calvin to be a rickshaw; a very small horseless buggy with two extended wooden arms set shoulder width apart.

In the moonlight, for just a moment, the young man saw a faint, soft glow emanating from the ancient woman. Then, as if imagined, it faded. He blinked, shook his head, and began to unload the packs from the canoe.

With a pack over each shoulder, Calvin followed as Esteen lifted the extended arms of the buggy and set off on a trail that led up and over the hill. Cresting the hill, the view just ahead opened up to a vast, overgrown piece of property. At the center, fifty yards away, stood a three-story white antebellum plantation home. Four Romanesque columns rose from a long marble porch, terminating at the third floor, and topped by a balcony which overlooked the bayou.

Although the surrounding land had fallen to neglect, not a window was broken. The porch was swept clean, as were the steps leading down to the circular drive, which showed signs of recent use.

The rickshaw stopped at the foot of the stairs, son leaned over to mother, and he carried her to a wheelchair waiting at the top. Calvin, following close behind, noted that this chair, although modern, bore the same coiled snake and alligator symbol etched into the push handles.

Speaking over her shoulder as Esteen began to wheel her towards her door, Miss Jovetta said, "Welcome to Lucielle. This house, and the property surrounding it, named after my grandmother's mother."

Esteen pushed open the ornate, eight-foot wooden double-doors, reached around the corner, flipped a light switch, and wheeled his mother across the threshold.

A grand chandelier illuminated an even grander receiving area. Twin white stone stairways rose in a bend following each wall to the second floor. At their feet, marble tiles covered every inch of the seven hundred square-foot foyer.

Lace drapes, tied back with gold rope, bordered the French windows set into each wall. Directly under the stairs was an archway leading to the kitchen, and to either side of the large room were arched doorways leading to other rooms.

For the first time in hours, Esteen spoke. "Take the gear upstairs to a bedroom, mon ami, and come meet us in the kitchen."

Doing as instructed, Calvin made his way to the nearest second floor room, set the gear down just inside and made his way down to the kitchen, his footfalls echoing around the large room.

Passing a window along the way, he saw headlights approaching from far down the road. Moving out of view, he chanced a look as the car rolled into the circular drive. On the passenger door, illuminated by the moonglow, he could make out the words CHALMETTE PARISH CORONER.

When the driver's door opened and the dome light came on, Calvin got a brief glimpse of a stunning young woman. She strode purposefully to the door and opened it.

The young man turned to see a young woman who, up to this point in Calvin's short life, was the most beautiful human being he had ever encountered.

Without pause, she came quickly across the room and threw herself into Esteen's arms. Dodging, Calvin had barely enough time to get out of the way.

Wordlessly, the auburn-haired angel hugged Esteen tightly. With eyes closed, the man returned the affection, lifting her from her feet.

Calvin, still nearby, could smell her as they embraced. A hint of perfume mixed with peach shampoo came to him. His eyes took in her lean form, dressed in a white cotton blouse, tan slacks, and low heels. Her cinnamon colored hair flowed to the middle of her back.

"Ah, Sophie!" Miss Jovetta said as she rolled into the foyer.

"Oh, Memaw!" the young lady said, as she pulled away from Esteen and dashed to the chair, leaning over and embracing the elder woman.

"Have you been feeding my Father?" Sophie said, as she buried her face in the old woman's hair. "He is losing weight. But I don't know how this could be. Who can resist your cooking?" she went on, planting kisses on her grandmother's head as she spoke.

"Oui mon cher, he eats well, but works ver' hard," Miss Jovetta responded. The grandmother's arms squeezed Sophie's neck as she spoke.

A couple silent moments passed. All parties wore pleasant smiles. Even Calvin, watching this stranger, couldn't help but grin. Life was happening.

"Sophie," Esteen said softly. "Turn and meet our guest, Calvin . . . we never asked, what is your last name?"

"Gasparilla," the young man said.

Esteen and Sophie gasped in unison at hearing the name Gasparilla. Calvin turned to Miss Jovetta who nodded her head, sighed and smiled.

6

"FAMILY TALK," MISS Jovetta announced to the room. Everyone followed her into the kitchen and gathered around the butcher-block table. The Matron of the family sat quietly waiting and smiling while Esteen, who all the while was looking intently at Calvin, poured chicory coffee for everyone and sat down. Sophie sat with her hands in her lap and looked wide-eyed back and forth between Miss Jovetta and the young man. Calvin felt the burn in his cheeks and wrung his sweaty hands, saying nothing and looking confused and nervous.

"Calvin Gasparilla," Miss Jovetta started, as she gently reached for his hand and held it, "Who is your father?"

"He was Thomas Gasparilla," the young man responded, looking at Esteen, who sighed deeply at the name. Miss Jovetta squeezed his hand gently.

"Why did you come to Louisiana?" she asked.

"Because my father mentioned how much he hated the place, he never said why. He would just say that whenever it came up on the T.V. I was going to New Orleans before . . . this happened."

"Everything happens for a reason," Miss Jovetta started, then looked at Esteen and said, "You tell the story, Mon cher."

Esteen leaned in closer across the table until he held Calvin's eyes and said, "I have a question for you, but before I ask it, let me tell you who you are." Esteen paused then, nodded as though he had made a decision and began.

"Your father, Thomas Gasparilla, is my fraternal twin brother, although we are nothing alike. I think he was born bad, even as a small child he was cruel."

This time it was Calvin who gasped, then listened wide-eyed as Esteen went on.

"When Thomas and I were twelve years old, he went into my father's room and killed him in his sleep. Shot him in the head with my father's own handgun.

I heard the shot and ran to the room and saw what he had done just as Thomas was crawling out the window. I cried out, "Why?!"

"Because I wanted to know what it felt like to

kill." Those were his last words and I never saw him again.

This was in 1944 and the law was different then. When I ran to the police station and told them what happened, they wouldn't believe me. A son just doesn't do that to his father and Rusk Gasparilla was a man with a good reputation and had always been respected as a single father.

The officer I talked to told my story to a detective on duty who decided, on the spot, that I was making things up because I hated my brother for some reason, and that this was a burglary gone wrong. The other son, poor boy, was probably afraid for his life and is running scared in the streets.

"You are my kin, my Nephew. There are forces bigger than us at work; those forces dropped you in our lap, oui? Everything happens for a reason.

"So, here is my question—you said that Thomas *was* your father. What happened to him?"

Calvin just breathed deeply, repeatedly, and stared into his lap, saying nothing for a long moment. He sobbed deeply then, racking sobs that came as quietly as he could manage. When he looked up, he looked Esteen in the eyes and said in a whisper, "I killed him!"

The words tumbled out of him, "He was real mean all the time, beat me sometimes. He tried to have sex with me one night a few months ago. Theresa, my sister, she warned me that he might, so I slept with a knife under my pillow." Calvin was talking faster and shaking so badly that his voice trembled and vibrated around the room. "And he came to me one night and I stabbed him in the heart!" He nearly yelled out the last sentence, then reflexively put his hands up to ward off a blow, but it didn't come.

Instead, when he looked at everyone around the room, he only saw kind eyes. Miss Jovetta and Sophie had tears running down their cheeks.

Esteen was calm and he gave a small smile that eased the young man, then gently said, "He was a rabid dog that had been hurting you your whole life. You just put him down. He was never a brother to me. You killed the man that was the kid that killed my father. It's a form of justice and it was the right thing to do, my Nephew."

"My Cousin," Sophie said gently.

Miss Jovetta reached for his hand and said," Mon cher, you are family."

LATER, SOPHIE ASKED Calvin about what happened the night before and they all listened as the seventeen-year old explained, leaving out none of the details.

When he finished, Sophie said, "The body will be found and will end up in my morgue. I will do the right thing to protect family."

Standing and grabbing Calvin's coffee cup, Esteen said, "No rest for you just yet." He poured a fresh cup for the young man and said, "Follow me out back. I will bring my cup and we will talk of the days to come."

Leaving Miss Jovetta and her granddaughter to talk in the kitchen, Calvin followed the older man as he led the way.

The back porch of the plantation home was sparse, and comfortable. Esteen lit a kerosene lamp, hung it from a near-by post, and directed the young man to a cushioned, handmade chair. The elder man sat across from him in a similar seat, and dragged a crate between them to put their cups on.

While Calvin sipped his bitter brew, Esteen brought out a pouch of tobacco, some papers, and began to roll a cigarette.

"Smoke with me, mon cher? It is what men do in our family for important palavers."

"Yes, Sir."

Deftly, Esteen rolled two cigarettes, handed one over to the young man, lit his own, and offered Calvin a light.

Inhaling, liking the man-to-man moment more than the smoke, Calvin coughed and pondered the meaning of the word "palaver."

The Louisiana night whispered its secrets, and both men listened. Time passed differently here. Long, wordless moments went by. At the far edge of the field before them, a twig snapped. A rustle in the bushes to their left drew Calvin's eyes, but the moonlight would not expose what the night held close.

Almost at a whisper, Esteen said, "When you hit that man, where did you learn that?"

"It was just what I did," Calvin said.

"Oui? it was the right move at the right time. I know it to be one of many strikes in a fighting style called Kenpo."

Both men finished their coffee. Awake now, the young man listened intently.

"My Sophie has learned this Kenpo, for many years now she has devoted much sweat, and sometimes pain, to become a third- degree black belt, and now is a Sensei-a teacher." Standing, the quiet man stepped to the porch rail and continued.

"You are not ready for this slow pace we have here. You are young, full of the future, but not prepared for it. If you will let us, my mother, Sophie, and I have much to teach you, each in our own way. What a man needs to know, I will show you. Sophie can prepare you for danger ahead, and my mother has the wisdom of generations, old ways hardly known in this age."

7

CALVIN WOKE IN what was the most comfortable bed he had ever been in. Three pillows surrounded his head. Beneath him, one foot deep, was a hand-made comforter that lay over a king-sized, hand stitched goose down mattress.

Esteen had shown him to one of many bedrooms after their late-night talk, and too exhausted to even turn on a light, he just set his pack by a wall, crawled into the moonlit bed in his boxer-shorts and passed out.

Late in the morning, Calvin sat up and surveyed the room. Behind him on the cypress headboard was the symbol that he had seen engraved on the handles of Miss Jovetta's chair, and on the bow of the canoe that he had paddled the night before; a water moccasin wrapped around an alligator. As he swung his feet to the hardwood floor, he made a mental note to ask about the meaning of this symbol.

He made his way to the bathroom and discovered a still steaming bath had been drawn for him. Slipping into the water he wondered but couldn't remember when he'd last bathed.

The smells of breakfast woke him from a catnap in the tub. After putting on his only clean shirt and pants, he made his way downstairs where he found Esteen and his mother sharing a quiet moment over coffee and beignets.

"Hooya, look here Mama. He lives," Esteen said with a smile as the young man took a seat with them at the butcher's block table.

Calvin smiled sheepishly at this, as his deep blue eyes searched the nearby stovetop for the source of the powerful aroma that dragged him stumbling down the stairs.

"You are hungry, mon cher?" Miss Jovetta said softly.

"Yes ma'am. I am."

His simple honesty brought a smile to her face. The ancient woman propelled her wheelchair to the stove and began filling a dish with red beans and rice, andouille, and eggs. Popping open the oven door, she drew a pan of biscuits, selected two, split them with a knife, laid them on a smaller plate and ladled sausage gravy over the top of them.

Laying them in her lap, she wheeled the plates to

the table and lay them before a boy trembling with hunger.

"Eat now, mon ami. This is the way we start each day. Mayhaps there will be no tomorrow." Wordlessly, Calvin dug in as she went on. "E'r day must be lived like it was yer last. Don't take your breath for granted, your vision, your hearing. These are gifts, given to us by He who wanted us to live another day."

Later in the afternoon, unaccustomed to the humidity and heat, Calvin struggled to keep pace with Esteen as they did chores around the plantation.

In its prime, the estate was a thriving vineyard. Generations of Robineuxs took pride in the fact that a slave never spent a day on their property. The daily operations were performed strictly by family members. Servants were handsomely paid to maintain the household. The vineyard still operated at 20% capacity. In the summer, Sophie tended to the pruning, and now at harvest time, Esteen and Calvin made preparations for the processing, and brought the winery up to working order for the year. Unable to do much more, Calvin watched, listened and helped when needed.

As the day wound to a close, Sophie met the men in the field with three glasses and a pitcher of sweet tea. They sat side-by-side on a bench on the shady side of the winery, while Sophie informed them that her "official cause of death" report as medical examiner for the parish stated that the driver in the crash that brought Calvin into their lives, had died of head and chest trauma stemming from the accident. Justice was served.

Minutes later, the three of them made their way to the house, where Miss Jovetta had chicken gumbo and corn bread waiting for them. The Robineuxs shared dinner and breezy conversation.

After a smoke together on the porch, Esteen instructed Calvin to pack a rope, a camping saw, gloves, and some hard bread into his duffel and load the gear into the canoe. The young man obeyed without question and met Esteen on the shore as the sun was setting.

With Calvin at the bow, Esteen pushed off from the shore into the darkening bayou. Paddling together, the craft made good time, slicing through the swamp scum and leaving a small wake. No moon lit their way, yet the young man found his vision adjusting to the darkness, and on occasion an incandescent green glow emanated from the Spanish moss which hung from the trees, reflected on the water, aiding navigation.

"Esteen, Sir," Calvin said, breaking the silence.

"Oui?"

"I was wondering about the snake and alligator symbol."

Nothing more needed to be said. There was a connection between them that made words seem like clutter.

"It is the crest of our family. You see that the snake does not have its teeth sunk into the 'gator's neck? They are not fighting." He explained, "They are bound together. They depend on the bayou for survival, but they are not enemies. A moccasin can't kill a gator, and a gator prefers fish to eat. It is in this way that we try to live. It is necessary sometimes to kill to survive, but we do not harm others like us. Savvy?"

Calvin nodded.

A moment later, Esteen pointed the canoe at a small island forested with a few small trees. On approach, Calvin swung into the water and pulled the canoe to shore. Esteen leaned forward, grabbed the duffel, threw it at the boy's feet, and dug his paddle into the water, dislodging the craft from shore, and leaving Calvin staring after him with unbelieving eyes and slack jawed.

"You have what you need, mon ami. Make your own way back to the house. Think, then do." Without another word of explanation, he turned and paddled into the thick darkness.

THINK, THEN DO. The boy reached into his duffel, withdrew the items he was told to pack and a flashlight.

Casting a beam on the trees available, he chose two and set to work with the camping saw, the flashlight gripped in his teeth. Cypress grew almost exclusively in the area and each tree was about thirty feet high. With gloves on he began to saw the nearest, cutting a wedge as he had seen Esteen do during their chores on the property. When the wedge was deep enough he stepped back, pushed and fell the tree into a clearing. After trimming the branches, he cut three ten-foot lengths and plopped to the ground exhausted. Although evening, the day's heat and humidity remained and taxed his energy.

He repeated the process with the other tree. Preparing to sit on a log for a moment, he glimpsed a shadow of movement, slow and narrow on the spot he had chosen to rest. Shining his light, he saw the snake come to a stop, then slide off and continue towards his leg. Jumping back, looking for his saw as a weapon, he paused as the snake made its way across the ground, moving away from him. "We kill to survive," he said aloud, as the reptile slithered away.

Out of danger but weary, he kept a close eye on his surroundings as he set four logs side by side. Cutting a fourth into two three-foot long pieces, he lay each new piece across the top and bottom of the four. Finding his rope, he laced it over and under the four and around the two on each end. Tying the loose ends, he flipped his raft and quickly found a sapling to cut as a push pole.

With great effort Calvin pushed the raft into the water, leaving an edge on shore. Repacking his duffel, he set it towards the front, dislodged the raft, and boarded it with push pole in hand. On his knees, he made his way back toward his family, using his memory and the faint remaining trail through the scum.

Moments into his trip, ahead and to his left, he saw the man-sized shadow of a gator leave a nearby shore and make its way toward him.

Think, then do. He reached into his pack and withdrew the hard bread and the saw. Gritting his teeth. he drew the saw across his forearm until it drew blood. He rubbed a large chunk of the bread in his blood, wound up, and threw it hard as he could behind the approaching gator. As the animal flipped in the water, Calvin dug his pole in deep, and doubled his speed toward home and family.

8

CALVIN STEPPED OFF into shallow water, with duffel in hand, before the raft hit shore. Making his way along the trail to the house he heard, "Calvin," whispered faintly from everywhere and nowhere.

"Come to me, mon cher." Clearly the whispered command was from Miss Jovetta. Looking up, he saw a pulsating blue glow emanating from the ancient woman's room.

Somehow, she was in his head. Unafraid and intrigued, he hurried into the house. Dropping his gear as he did so, he rapidly made his way up the winding stone stairway to her room.

"Come."

The blue glow was fading as he entered. The antique furniture, hardwood floors, and four poster bed were returning to normal shades, and by the window facing the bayou, Miss Jovetta sat facing him in her wheelchair. Her gnarled hands folded and resting on an afghan laid over her lap, she smiled sweetly as he approached.

"Why are you here, cher?" she asked.

"Because you called me, Ma'am."

"Hmmm . . . why did you hear me?"

Buying time, the young man grabbed a nearby stool and moved it close to her. Sitting, he took a full minute to answer.

"Because . . ." he began tentatively, ". . . I don't really know."

"Are you angry at Esteen for leaving you?" she asked.

"No, Ma'am."

"Why?"

Again he paused.

"Because, he would not put me in danger without a way out. He told me to pack what I would need. He . . . cares for me."

The blue light flashed from her eyes and was gone. He had seen just a glimpse of the same light in her eyes as they were leaving the bayou shack to come here, and again more brilliantly when he came to shore.

The mysterious matron of the Robineux family smiled broadly, showing her unlikely white teeth.

"Oui! Oui! You are . . . tuned into us. You do not

hear other voices in your head, because you are not crazy. Only I can reach you this way. You hear because we, all of us, are entwined. I am a telepath, you understand? As was my grandmother. It is my gift now, and I reach out to family only. In emergencies, or if one of us dies, will be the only time you will experience this. This night, I do this to show you, and it has taken ver' much energy. Help me to bed, little one," her voice weakening as she finished.

Offering his arm, she grabbed it and together they made it to her bed. As he covered her, she gently pecked him on the cheek, lay back, and closed her eyes.

9

CALVIN WOKE TO music the next morning. He dressed and followed the Zydeco melodies to the back porch. Esteen was working the keys of an accordion and smiling at Sophie as she sawed a lively tune on a fiddle. Miss Jovetta worked a wooden spoon up and down a washboard perched on her lap.

The young man had never seen an instrument played, and sat down nearby, watching in awe as the family made festive music together on the sunlit porch. Esteen let out an "Aiyee!" and they all stopped on the next beat.

Calvin smiled broadly and clapped as they all took a bow.

"Let's eat!" Sophie said. Esteen grabbed the push-handles of his mother's chair and wheeled her into the kitchen. An egg sandwich and a bowl of cheese-grits were set at each place, and they all ate in silence. When the meal was finished, the family formed a circle, inviting Calvin to join hands with them. After a moment of silence the grandmother, son, and his daughter said in unison, "Camille."

Esteen broke away, and quickly disappeared into another room.

Sophie motioned for Calvin to follow her as she led the way out the back door and around the house to the road.

"Walk with me a bit," she said quietly, and side by side they made their way down the road. After a few moments she said, "The music this morning was a celebration of my mother's life. Speaking her name, Camille, was in memory of her death. Today is the thirteenth anniversary of her passing. Father wasn't always such a quiet man. When they were together, their laughter was music, and when they kissed the stars shone a little brighter. Fifteen years they had together until the day Mother went shopping in New Orleans for an anniversary dress. A dead-soul-walking took her life in a department store restroom. He violated her, stabbed her to death, and took her eyes." She paused and Calvin saw her face contort into a mask of hate. Her once brilliant green eyes were mere slits, and her fists became clubs.

He walked a step behind her, letting her work it out, as they approached an out-building by the side of the road. She opened the weatherworn wooden door, and motioned for him to go in.

Skylights in the vaulted ceiling provide daylight to the building . . . The floor was totally covered in interlocking foam mats. A long heavy rope hung in the center of the room. High up on a mirrored wall was a shelf of trophies and framed achievement awards, and on one end of that wall a heavy bag hung from a beam. On the other end were a bench and a rack of free weights. To their right was a small room, and to the left of the door were two coat hooks. Each had a white, lightweight top hanging from them, and under each a pair of matching drawstring pants lay folded.

Sophie grabbed a top, reached down for some pants, and handed them to Calvin.

"This is a Gi. Put it on in that little room, while I change here. Today you will be beat-up by a girl," she said with a grin and a wink.

When Calvin had finished changing, he found Sophie standing in the middle of the room. She motioned for him to join her and led him through some stretching and range of motion exercises.

During the warm-up, Sophie explained; "I've been training in Kenpo since Mother was taken from us. My only motivation was revenge, hoping I would somehow find the thing that killed my mother, and exterminate it. The crime was random, and with no witnesses or trace evidence, the police came up empty in their investigation. When I was sixteen, after they had classified it a cold case, I left Father against his wishes and went to New Orleans to try to find the killer. I had heart but no skills, and almost no money. The street people hurt me, in ways Father will never know. One night, a uniformed police officer cuffed me, threw me in his car, and violated me on the shores of Lake Pontchartrain. I had only been training in Kenpo for a year and wasn't able to stop him."

She paused for a moment to show Calvin a different stretching technique, and went on, "I came home the next day and found Mr. Townsend, my Sensei—which means teacher. I told him what happened, made him promise not to tell Father, and begged for more intense, severe training. He agreed to this and spent the next five years showing me all that he knew. Beyond the standard training, he gave me his secrets. All Senseis have them; maybe one student in their dojo will learn them. I was that student."

Then she attacked Calvin. Pulling her blows, she struck and kicked him, careful not to use fatal techniques. She hit the surprised student in every exposed quadrant of his body, backing him up, but never taking him to the mat.

"Fight me! Swing. Kick. Stop me!" she hissed.

He tried swinging at her and she easily blocked him. When he kicked, she parried. Allowing him to back her up, she deflected his unskilled attempts, sidestepped his charges, and eventually swept his legs, leaving him on his back, gasping for breath.

"I am NOT a girl. Not here," she said quietly while he tried to catch his breath.

"Don't try to treat me like one. You have no skill, but you have heart and superior strength. You were torn between defending yourself and being worried about hurting me. You can't hurt me. Not yet." She offered him a hand up. He rejected it and started shaking, his eyes watering. He paced around her wearily.

"Why did you do that?! I thought we . . . I don't know, fuck!" He sobbed as adrenaline surged through him.

He couldn't stop pacing. Walking away from her, he punched the heavy bag, sending it arching back. Stepping to the weight rack, he grabbed a dumbbell and sent it crashing into the mirrored wall. Not sated, all the pain and anger of his life surfacing at that moment, he continued grabbing weights and smashing them into the mirrors. Sobbing, making guttural noises, he threw them all and began pummeling the hanging mirror shards with his fists. Groaning in pain, shreds of skin hanging from his knuckles, he continued until all his strength bled out of him, and he fell to his knees. His head bowed and his chin rested on his chest while the blood streamed from his damaged knuckles, soaking the mat.

Sophie walked into the small room where Calvin had changed and returned with a first-aid kit. She knelt beside him and gently cleaned his damaged knuckles. No words passed between them as she continued to apply first aid, and wrap his hands in gauze, then tape.

Sophie said, "I'm sure you were told, 'Think, then do,' by my father, as he has told me many times. He saw that you understood and was confident that you would return from the island. I say, 'Think fast, react quickly, and you'll live to see another sunrise. I think you'll leave us soon. You are a noble soul, Grandmother sees it. I do too. You have been a victim, but you fought the good fight. Train with me, and I will give you all that I have in the time we are together. Do you trust me?"

"Sort of," Calvin said, rising.

"Do you understand what just happened?"

"I do now. You were preparing me for the unexpected," he said as he faced her.

He flinched as she leaned in to hug him, stepping back as she did it. Seeing that she was off balance, he stepped back again quickly and grinned as she fell to her knees. Sophie leaned on her right knee, swept her left foot out, connected with the back of his right leg, and he fell to the mat.

Calvin began to chuckle, and Sophie joined him. Soon they were both bent over, laughing hysterically. Helping each other up, laughing and wiping tears, they leaned on each other, catching their breath together. A bond was made, forged by the fire they both had inside, and hard as steel.

Sophie led him through a Kata; repetition of blocks, blows, and footwork that, when done smoothly, looked like a lethal dance. Mindful of his sore hands, she continued to train with him for another hour, answering any questions he had and talking him though the movements.

They went their separate ways to change, and when Calvin came back, Sophie held out a patch, showing him.

"No belt for you, Brother. That's not what we're doing here, but this patch, Moccasin and Gator, means you are now my best student." And with a wink she said, "And the only one."

10

MISS JOVETTA WAS on the back porch when Sophie and Calvin returned to the house. When they were near enough for her grandmother to hear, Sophie said, "I heard the Jeep go by when we were changing, is he . . . ?"

"Oui. Esteen went to find Camille's eyes."

Sophie sat on a stool next to her, put a hand on her shoulder, and said, "Oh. Memaw. Don't fret. We knew that he would. It's 'The Day.'"

Quietly they held each other, and Calvin left them that way. He went into the house and out the front door. Just off to the right side of the house, the bay door of a shed stood open. In the distance, he could see dust still hovering over the road.

Sophie was alone in the kitchen when he came back in. They sat together quietly at the table. For a few minutes she didn't acknowledge him, just stared out the window, watched her grandmother sit alone on the porch.

"We used to go together, Father and me," she finally said.

"After I had come home from my time in the city, we both agreed that we had to try to find out who did it. At first, we would go into the city every weekend. We would start at the department store, trying to find new witnesses, looking around the area for a murder weapon, anything that would bring us closer to an answer. We would stay at a motel and spend the weekend going over the facts of the case, reviewing reports that the police gave us. I was so young, and Father was out of his league. But we had to try. Had to do something, anything, to make sense of it all."

She shook her head slowly and paused. Calvin got up, grabbed two bottles of water and returned to the table, setting one in front of her. He sat down again and waited for her to work it out, knowing there was more.

Sophie grabbed the bottle, stood, and began to pace around the room.

She began again. "After a while, our trips were fewer and fewer, until eventually it became an annual pilgrimage that Father carried on without me. I went on to college, got a degree in forensic medicine, and eventually ended up as the M.E. for the parish.

I hoped that maybe somehow, in the course of my cases, that I would find evidence that this freak had a pattern, other victims. Something to go on. In time I realized how morbid that was, waiting for another body to turn up on my watch."

"When will he be back?" Calvin said.

She stopped pacing, held his eyes for a long moment, seeing his distress, and said, "Don't worry, Brother. He's not in danger, just doing what he must. Tomorrow, maybe the next day, he'll come back to us."

From the porch, a low moan carried into the kitchen. They both turned to the window at the sound. Miss Jovetta was leaning heavily to one side, her wispy hair hanging over the arm of the wheelchair. Sophie bolted for the door, Calvin on her heels.

"Memaw?!" Sophie cried as they came through the door. The ancient woman was breathing, but the left side of her face was contorted in what looked like a death rictus. Her right eye was abnormally wide open, while the left was squeezed shut.

Calvin watched as Sophie straightened her grandmother's body in the chair. Her breathing was shallow, and her open eye did not register movement as the medically trained young woman checked her pulse, held her head and looked deeply into the open eye.

"Stroke," Sophie said, quickly gathered her grand-mother in her arms and rushed her past Calvin, through the door.

"My keys in my purse! Get them!" she said over her shoulder as she continued toward the front door. Calvin grabbed the purse and quickly followed them to the car, digging for the key and finding them.

"Can you drive?" she asked.

"No."

"Damn! Come around the other side, sit and hold her steady on your lap, don't let her roll. I will be driving fast!"

Calvin rushed to the far side of the car, threw the keys and purse on the front seat, got in and helped her get the old woman settled. He cradled her head and shoulders on his lap as Sophie came around, shut his door, got in, started the car and deftly spun out of the circular drive and down the dirt road. Sophie got on her cell phone as they drove.

11

AFTER TWO DAYS of observation at Lafayette Medical Center, Miss Jovetta was sent home in Sophie's care.

The matriarch of the Robineux family was unable to talk, and only had the use of her right arm. The Neurologist at LMC assured Sophie that in time, with round the clock care and months of speech and physical therapy, her grandmother would likely regain her speech and at least some use of her left arm.

Esteen returned a day later and immediately took on the responsibility of caregiver. He never spoke of his trip to the city. In fact, he was even quieter than was his nature, and only spoke when asked a question ...

FOR THE NEXT two months, Calvin remained with

his family. Well-fed and gaining muscle from taking on double the daily chores, he had become a man.

After work and on her days off, his sister continued to train with him at every opportunity. She was also adept at Krav Maga and taught him how to disarm a person wielding a knife or a gun. A quick learner, Calvin soon earned hard won praise from Sophie. She was relentless, often pushing him to frustration and exhaustion. Beyond the physical aspect of the martial arts, she schooled him in the ancient ways of integrating mental and spiritual control. Late in the evenings, long after the others had gone to bed, the two warriors faced each other on the mats. Legs folded and eyes closed, the teacher helped the student find his calm center.

Still a teenager, Calvin had already killed two men. Rage, guilt, and turmoil were seated deep in his psyche; Sophie walked him out of the guilt in their meditation sessions and helped him channel—rather than release—the rage. Justice demanded focused rage, she told him. Without that drive, only the intellect remained; and it was not enough to keep the fire burning.

A small crew was hired to harvest the vineyard, and with that done, Calvin became restless. Household chores were becoming his, often being left alone at the plantation while Esteen transported Miss Jovetta to her therapy appointments.

While hanging laundry, a slip of paper fell out of one of Esteen's shirts. Calvin picked up the soggy newspaper clipping and unfolded it carefully. It was an article from the Times -Picayune about a recent unsolved murder. A woman had been found dead in Pirates Alley. She had been raped, stabbed to death, and her eyes were missing. Below the article was a follow-up piece about the District Attorney filing a motion to suppress any more details of the case being released to the press, and that he would pursue filing charges against the investigative reporter, Jacob Turpin, demanding that he reveal the source that leaked the information about the missing eyes.

At the top of the article, Esteen had written a name, Aldo Muncie, and a question mark. Calvin carefully laid the article on the porch railing to dry and made a decision.

12

THAT EVENING, WHILE the family was gathered for a dinner of gar fish patties, red beans and rice, and corn bread, Calvin said, "It's my birthday tomorrow. I'll be eighteen."

"Mawmin an adawt," Miss Jovetta said.

Esteen nodded and said, "Oui, Calvin's an adult momma. But he been a man for a while now, for sure."

With that, the elder man put his hand on Calvin's shoulder and gave it a squeeze. Sophie leaned in from the other side and wrapped her arm around her cousin's shoulders.

"A strong man, with a lion's heart," she said with a beaming smile.

Calvin grinned, blushed, and looked down at his plate. He relished the praise, but in a moment his smile faded.

"I will leave here tomorrow." The young man was

unaccustomed to making dramatic statements, and
he struggled to find the right words. No-one broke
the silence, letting him work it out. When he looked
up, all eyes were on him as he continued, "I am happy
to be with family, and we are in each other, but I'm
restless. I saw a little of the world before you met me,
and it's calling me."

"I am not surprised," Esteen said, and turned to
face Calvin squarely.

"I am ver' sorry I have not been saying much
lately. But I have been seeing the wanderlust in you."
Miss Jovetta nodded when he finished. Calvin saw a
rapid blue flash in her eyes, and then it was gone just
as quickly.

"Ming!" The ancient woman said, looking at Sophie.

"Oui, Memaw," Sophie said. She got up, left the
room. and a moment later she came back and set a
small cypress box on the table in front of Calvin.

"Open it, Cousin," she said.

He lifted the lid and saw a silver ring on a patch
of royal blue velvet, the moccasin and gator symbol
crafted on the face of it. For a long moment he gazed
at it, and a lump formed in his throat.

"This house, this land, is a safe place for us. But,
out there in the world it's different," Sophie said as
she lifted the ring from the box and reached for Cal-

vin's right hand. Slipping it on his ring finger, she continued, "It fits you well. Father made it for you with silver that Memaw held while calling to you from the shore with her mind. A bit of us all is in it."

"Tomorrow," Esteen said, "We gather and make music for my nephew." For the first time, Calvin saw him smile at him the way he did when they had come out of the swamp and Sophie entered the house.

WHEN MORNING CAME, Esteen looked through the kitchen window and saw Calvin on the back porch. His duffel was packed and leaning against the rail.

Esteen brought out two steaming cups of chicory coffee and took a seat next to him. They rolled smokes together, and sat quietly drinking, smoking, and enjoying each other's company.

"I found this," Calvin said as he handed him the newspaper clipping. "It fell out of your shirt."

Esteen nodded, unfolded it, and read it again briefly.

"This man who wrote it," Esteen said, "Jacob Turpin. I met with him. I told him about Camille and he told me the name of that suspect, Aldo Muncie. Said Muncie had been in Angola on a rape/assault charge all these years. That the woman in that case escaped, and now Muncie is free. Turpin made me promise not to tell anyone about this name because he got it from a cop who would lose his job for telling him."

Esteen's gunmetal grey eyes narrowed and he asked, "Will you go to New Orleans from here?"

"Yes Sir."

"Be e'r so careful, cher."

"I will."

Sophie came out pushing Miss Jovetta, who had a fiddle and bow in her lap. An accordion hung from a push handle swinging behind her.

Esteen rose, grabbed the accordion and slung it on. Sophie grabbed the fiddle and bow, then nodded at her father. They agreed on a medley and began to play.

Soon the late summer morning was filled with the sound of Louisiana, as interpreted by the Robineuxs. Miss Jovetta tapped out a beat on the arm of her chair with her right hand, smiling a crooked smile.

Calvin tapped his feet as the musicians played though their medley, alternating slowly and fast tunes. With an "Aiyee!" from Esteen, they finished on the down beat.

Sophie looked toward the duffel as she laid her instrument down on a bench. Her grandmother followed her gaze, and the matriarch made a low, sad sound.

Calvin rose then, walked to Miss Jovetta, leaned down and gave her a long hug. When they separated, she looked deeply into his wet eyes, nodded, and said softly, "It's time."

No-one was hungry, so no breakfast was made. Sophie offered to drive Calvin to New Orleans, and they all made their way to the front of the house and out onto the marble porch.

Esteen held out his hand, shook Calvin's firmly, and said nothing.

Sophie popped the trunk, tossed Calvin's gear in, and reached into her purse. She handed him ten one-hundred-dollar bills and said, "Until you find work."

They both got in the car. Calvin waved at his family, and his sister piloted the car down the road and eventually out of sight.

13

NEW ORLEANS. CALVIN had been through a few cities, but as they approached this one, he couldn't help feeling dread.

Sophie brought him to the motel row on Airline Highway. She waited as he paid cash at the Hummingbird Motel for a week's rent. No I.D. was required.

When they drove around to the back they hugged, she pecked him on the cheek, gave him her cell number and reminded him of his training, and to keep his center intact.

"Don't lose it, Brother. Keep the fire burning, but don't let it consume you."

They parted. Calvin watched until her car was out of sight, turned, and brought his duffel into his room. It was small, with a worn brown carpet. It smelled like mildew, and the dark color of the carpet didn't quite hide the stains. The bed was big, and the sheets were crisp.

There was a T.V. bolted to the wall, and a remote sitting on the bedside stand. Calvin turned it on and listened to the midday news report on a local channel. It had been months since he had seen a T.V. and he enjoyed the distraction. He missed the escape television had provided during his dark youth. Movies were his salvation when his biological father was in a drunken rage. As long as he stayed glued to the set and didn't make eye contact with the human called his father, things went better for him. He thought about the last time he'd seen that man alive and turned up the volume to drown out the memory.

The talking heads on the T.V. were discussing the aftermath of Katrina. Calvin had heard something about the hurricane that had destroyed the Ninth Ward, and reduced the population of the city from 2,000,000 to 500,00 people, but it meant nothing to him.

He turned the channel, found one of his favorite action movies, and lay down on the bed. Remembering his shoes, he leaned over to untie them and heard the crackle of paper in his pants pocket. He reached in and removed the newspaper article. Laying it next to him, he untied his shoes, kicked them off, and re-read the entire piece.

The movie droned on, and he forgot about it as he went over the details of the article. It was why he was here. His family needed him to do this. Sophie had her career, and Esteen was taking care of his mother full-time now.

He lay down on the pillow, the exhaustion of the day's emotions catching up to him. As he drifted off, the names rattled around in his brain; Jacob Turpin, reporter, Aldo Muncie, the killer? What was the name of the detective feeding Turpin the information?

IT WAS DARK when someone knocked and woke him from a dreamless nap. The television was still droning on when he opened his eyes. The blue glow lit his way as he stepped to the peep hole.

A teen black girl stood nervously outside. She looked left, right, and behind her like a bird watching for a predator, then turned to the door and raised a hand to knock again.

Calvin cracked the door and said, "Yes?"

"Do Tre be up in there?"

"No, sorry," he said. As he pushed the door shut, she expertly caught it with her foot.

"Whoa whoa. Wait up!" She smiled big when he opened the door farther.

"Ooo you got pretty dark bangs! An' them eyes! You sure you don't need some comp'ny?" the under-age girl purred.

"No. Thank you." He pushed the door shut.

Turning toward the bed, he took a step and heard the shuffle of feet outside. Alerted, he paused to listen when another knock came. Without checking the peephole, he turned the knob and the door exploded inward.

Calvin's trained instinct took over as he stepped to the side, his left hand grabbed the intruder's wrist that held the gun, bent it down and forced the hand open as the thug's momentum took him in an arc toward the bed. Calvin's right came up and knife-edged down hard on the neck of his attacker, causing the man's head to ricochet off the corner of the bed and down to the floor.

Calvin heard the girl's steps as she ran off, but his eyes never left the person on the floor before him as he reached down and grabbed the gun. Unfamiliar with guns, he fumbled a little but was soon able to dislodge the clip and put it in his pocket. He pulled the slide back and checked the chamber, grinning as he mentally thanked Sophie for covering this in his training.

The skinny young man on the floor rose to his

knees slowly. He shook his head and the pain made him cry out.

Backing up as he got up rubbing his neck, he said, "Damn, white boy! Ouch! Fuck! You knocked me out!"

"Yup," Calvin said and handed him his gun. He pointed toward the open door and the unforgiving streets of New Orleans beyond the parking lot and said, "Go play somewhere else."

14

CALVIN WAS RESTLESS. He called the *Times-Picayune* offices, got routed through to Turpin's extension, and left a message on the voice mail. He asked for an appointment and left his room number.

He needed clothes and a haircut. The haircut would have to wait a day, but he knew he could get clothing at a twenty-four-hour big box store. He called a taxi and made an appointment for thirty minutes later, then dug out a light-weight short sleeved buttoned-down shirt and his best jeans and took them to the bathroom, hanging them on a hook to steam while he took a shower.

As the hot water cascaded over his newly muscled back, he mentally chastised himself for standing in front of the door when he answered the first time. If the street-thug had been there first, he might have caught a bullet. On the second knock, he turned the knob and had his door kicked in. He made a mental note to ask who's there while standing to the side. Think, then do.

At ten p.m. he got in the cab and told the driver what he needed. His driver was a young black guy, just a few years older than him, with an easy-going talkative personality. There was a strong-smelling steaming cup of coffee in the drink holder, and Amos Lee was delivering a smooth groove on the CD player.

The nearest store was outside the city in Metairie, and Calvin gave the driver mental points for taking what seemed to be the most direct route.

"My name's Chris," the driver said as they rolled along.

"I'm C . . . Vin," Calvin answered.

"Wassat?"

"Vin, my name's Vin."

He was eighteen now. The name Calvin always reminded him of a comic-strip, and he thought Vin sounded . . . stronger.

"Pleased to meet you, Vin. Hey, you got a cell? You got a cell; you can call me when you need to be picked up."

"No, I don't."

"Man, you gonna need one. If you got the bills, you should pick one up at the store."

"Yeah. I'll do that."

They pulled up to the front of the store, and Chris gave him a card with his number on it. Vin reached into his pocket to pay the fare, and pulled out hundreds. The dome light was on and Chris saw the money come out.

"Damn, Vin. No small bills huh? I can break a Benjamin but look: it ain't safe bringin' them out like that around the city. You oughta get 'em broke down when you're in there."

"Thanks I will. Really. Thank you. You're a cool guy," Vin said.

"Sho yo right! Don't you forget neither," the driver said with a big smile.

An hour later, Vin was back in the cab. He'd bought a cell phone with 500 minutes, and clothing and shoes for all occasions.

He was still restless, so he had the cabbie, whom he nicknamed Smilin' Chris, wait to give him a ride to the famous French Quarter.

On the way from motel row, they passed the newly restored Superdome standing silently in the dark. Angling toward Canal Street, the cab passed a cemetery, and unique above ground tombs held Vin's attention.

Chris commented on the way by that, for the tourist's sake, the graveyard was better lit than the Superdome. "That's Nawlins way of sayin' welcome," Chris said with his trademark smile.

Even though it was night, and the windows were closed, the oppressive humidity of the city seeped into the taxi as they slowed down and entered the central business district. They turned into the Quarter off Rampart Street, and Vin mentioned the stench coming into the car, "It smells like mildew and . . . I don't know what. Must still be cleaning up from the hurricane, huh?"

Chris laughed out loud at that and said, "Nah, the Quarter didn't get hardly no damage. It always smell like piss, puke, shrimp, and oysters. We'll start worryin' if it ever smells like Pine-Sol." Just as he finished saying this, he rolled to a stop on the corner of Bourbon and St. Ann.

"End of the road," he said. "Can't cross Bourbon at night 'cause they got the street barricades up."

He turned, winked at Vin and said, "So you goin' to get tore-up drunk tonight?"

"I've never had a drink," Vin said. "But maybe I will."

"You never . . ." Smilin' Chris stared for moment, his mouth agape.

Vin looked calmly back at him. Another moment passed like that, both young men holding their expressions. Slowly, Chris began to grin. His eyes sparkled, the grin becoming a charming toothy smile.

15

VIN HAD BEEN though a few cities, hung out in a couple, but nothing in his travels had prepared him for the French Quarter of New Orleans. From St. Ann street he headed south on Bourbon and through the looking glass.

Tourists staggered and strolled down the middle of the street. Most were holding drinks in plastic cups, while others watched the show that the revelers put on. The crooked, broken pavement added to the entertainment as humans tripped and tipped along. No building stood more than four stories high. Each one was of Spanish and French architecture, with wrought iron railings wrapped around second and third story balconies that supported hotel guests who looked down at the less fortunate while they drank and pointed.

Music poured from every door along the way. Vin

stopped and listened when he heard Zydeco coming from inside The Court of Two Sisters. The melodies made him feel something he had never experienced before; he was homesick. He reminded himself to call Sophie first thing the next morning, and quickly strode down the street, putting distance between himself and that brand of music.

A fantastic aroma coming from a place called Buster's reminded Vin that he hadn't had dinner, and drew him through the swinging doors. A stunning hostess greeted him and escorted him to a table along a wall far from the funk of the street outside.

The restaurant was painted in gaudy shades of purple, gold, and green and the customers ranged from low budget travelers to high powered businessmen and women. All present were in good spirits, and a live jazz band in the corner kept the mood upbeat.

When his waitress came by, Vin ordered a Hurricane, his first alcoholic drink, and a sampler platter of Oysters Rockefeller, Oysters Creole, and Oysters Manhattan, all baked on the half-shell.

His dinner proved to be one of the best he'd ever had, and the twenty-four ounce Hurricane, now half empty, was fast becoming his favorite drink. He liked the fuzzy feeling of his first buzz. Colors seemed brighter, the waitress was getting cuter, and the musicians were now semi-gods.

Vin polished off the last twelve ounces of his drink without pausing for a breath and stood. His knees betrayed him and the table he was leaning on gave way. From his new vantage point on the floor, the ceiling fan became a new enemy, causing his world to spin out of control.

Vin was lifted to his feet by a couple employees, paid his bill, and was escorted out the door by the doorman. Music. lights, laughter, and the stench of the Quarter hit him all at once. He rushed around the corner and left his dinner on someone's doorstep. But he wanted more.

He had rarely let himself feel, and when he did it had been explosive. Now he felt it all. The abuse, the neglect, the killing. Vin, a "man" now, wanted to hurt someone. Anyone. Bad.

He found Johnny White's, a hangout for bikers, dealers, and professional drinkers. Tourists were not welcome, and soon realized it if they made the mistake of finding the joint.

Vin walked up to the scarred pine bar and asked for something strong. The bartender was a pro, and read the fire in his eyes. He poured a double-shot of rum with a splash of coke for coloring and slid it to him.

Vin paid with a twenty. A thirty something hooker caught the action from down the bar and got up from her seat, eyes locked on-target. Halfway there, the bartender caught her eye and shook his head. She mouthed the words "Fuck off," and started again.

"Sheree! No," he hissed through his teeth and caught her shoulder.

"Aww. Jimmy! Damn! Look at him! He's soo ready."

Jimmy kept a hold of her shoulder and glared, "No."

Sheree did her best pout, turned, and headed back to her perch. Vin caught it all. He downed his drink in one toss, and said, "Jimmy."

"Yeah."

"It's Jimmy, right?"

"Yeah."

"Give me another drink, please, and one for the lady."

Sheree perked up. "See? He even said please."

"Buddy," Jimmy sneered, "Nobody says please here, and she ain't no lady."

Vin motioned for the bartender to come closer. Jimmy poured him another double, walked over and leaned in.

Two fingers hooked him by the nostrils and

tugged his face down to the bar. Vin whispered, "Cool; now I know the rules."

When Vin released him, Jimmy threw a round-house. Vin caught the forearm coming in, applied his thumb to a pressure point, and dragged the slow learner back down to the bar.

"What?" Vin said through his teeth. "Something else you wanted to tell me?"

"Nnno!" Jimmy squealed.

"Ah, good."

Sheree landed on the stool next to him and said, "Jimmy. Sweetie. How about you quit hasslin' my new friend and get me a Long Island."

Vin released him again, and he staggered back-wards and out of reach. Without a word, the bar-tender turned and started making the hooker a drink.

With her nails running a trail up his thigh, she said to Vin, "What's your name, baby?"

"Doesn't matter, ma' . . ." He started to say ma'am and caught himself.

"Sure. OK. Whatever . . ." She let it trail off.

Red faced, Jimmy slammed her drink down, grabbed a ten from Vin's stack of change, and mum-bled, "Jus' tryin' to do you a favor, buddy."

Vin didn't respond.

Outside of some clumsy moments when he was younger, he had never been with a woman. His dark

hair and blue eyes got him plenty of attention growing up, but he ignored the signals and left the girls
irritated.

He wanted sex, but not with this one.

"So," Sheree tried again, "You want some company tonight?"

He politely told her no and walked out the door
into the madness.

His change disappeared from the bar before his
feet hit the sidewalk.

Vin found another bar and drank until his head
was swimming.

He dug out the phone number of Smilin' Chris,
called him and waited. This was not his town. Not
who he was.

16

VIN WOKE UP fully dressed half on, half off the bed and feeling barely alive. His stomach was on fire, his head felt too big to lift, and his eyelids hurt.

He slid the rest of the way to the floor and began crawling toward the shower. When he crossed the threshold to the bathroom, the phone rang. It sounded like a freight train and needed to be stopped before it killed him.

Reversing course, he crawled, stumbled, and leaped for the phone on the nightstand. As he lifted the receiver, it slipped from his grasp and tumbled to the floor. He leaned down to pick it up, and his brain sloshed forward, causing him excruciating pain and dropping him to his knees. He grabbed the receiver, said "Hello?" and curled up in the fetal position on the brown, stained carpet.

"Yes um . . ." The voice on the other end hesitated.

"Calvin Robinuex?"

"Vin. Call me Vin." The words came out like a gasp and a moan.

"Well, Ok, Vin. This is Jacob Turpin. I got your message, and I'm able to meet with you today at say . . . one o'clock. I'll be in the lounge at Harrah's."

"One. Yes. OK. Thank you, Mr. Turpin. See you then," Vin managed.

"Ok . . . are you alright, Vin? If you're sick we can . . ."

"No! No. Sorry. Please, I'll be there at one." Vin reached up, hung up, and did a slow shoulder roll in the direction of the shower. It was noon.

Vin came out of the shower feeling a little closer to alive than dead. He put on a white Polo shirt, some beige Dockers, and some Earth Shoe sandals. Checking himself in the mirror, he was satisfied with the casual look, but cursed himself for not getting a haircut. It would have to do. He called Chris for a ride.

VIN SAID, "HARRAH'S," then slid into the passenger seat and lay down.

"You goin' to break the house now, huh new fish?" Chris said, a little too loud on purpose.

The casualty in the backseat didn't respond.

The smiling cabbie chuckled his way out of the parking lot, and deftly piloted the car into the stream of day dwellers.

Fifteen minutes later, Chris rolled under the canopy of the casino, and stomped the brakes.

Vin was ready for it, his hands already gripping the back of the passenger seat. He got out, threw a twenty through the window, grinned a little at the driver and said, "You know you suck, right?"

"Yes, yes I do." Chris smiled proudly and pulled away.

The bar was empty at Harrah's except for an elderly woman staring off into space with a fruity drink in her hand, and a fortyish man wearing a tie and rolled-up shirtsleeves. Vin sat down next to the man and introduced himself.

Jacob Turpin shook his hand briskly, and at the same time assessed Vin in a sweeping glance. Vin was doing the same.

At the offer of a drink, Vin grimaced and opted for a coffee. He accepted an offered cigarette and smoked in silence as the investigative reporter took a minute to finish tapping buttons on his BlackBerry.

"You don't look like your uncle," the reporter said.

"I know." Vin sipped his coffee.

With a polite but loaded smile, Jacob said, "I

know you'll understand then, that I need to see your driver's license. Just a precaution."

"I don't have one," Vin said. He went on, "Long story really, but I don't have any I.D. No social security card, state I.D., credit cards, I don't even own a wallet." He realized how it sounded, but the fact was that he came from nomadic roots and had never had occasion or need to get what other citizens considered mandatory to survive in society.

Turpin looked long and hard at him. "Just a moment. You father gave me your sister's number, she's an M.E., right? I'll call her and have her confirm your identity for me."

Sophie. Vin missed her more than ever.

Turpin made the call while Vin finished his coffee and asked for a refill. At this time of day the casino wasn't doing much business, but the few slot machines that were being played near the bar were making enough noise to keep Vin's head pounding. When the bartender returned with his coffee, Vin asked for an aspirin chaser.

"She says you have a ring," Turpin said when he'd finished his call. "I don't see one."

The ring. Vin had been carrying it in his pocket. Not used to wearing one, he had occasionally been rubbing it like a worry stone over the last couple days.

He dug it out, put it on, and held it out for the reporter to look at.

"Snake around a gator. Never seen anything like that before," Turpin said.

Vin just nodded. His politeness was fading by the hour. Being on his own again was different this time. There were monsters lurking in the shadows, and his guard was always up. Things were changing. He was changing.

"Aldo Muncie," Vin said. "My father wrote that name above an article you wrote about the murder in Pirate's Alley. Who is this guy?"

"Bad guy. Real bad guy," Turpin said. "Went down on a first-degree assault/ attempted rape charge. Got out of Angola a while ago after doing a thirteen-year bit." He offered Vin another smoke and lit it for him.

"What did you tell my father about Muncie that got him to write his name down?."

The reporter's eyes narrowed. He didn't answer right away, took a moment to sip his drink and take a few drags of his cigarette.

Vin didn't mind waiting, never had. The aspirin was kicking in, and the coffee was fresh. He was feeling better by the moment.

"Listen . . ." Turpin hesitated, and went on, "Muncie had a cellmate a few years ago. The guy was up for parole and thought that telling the board something that Muncie had said would help him with his chances of getting out." He paused again. "I'm not supposed to know this, I have an unnamed source on the board. During this guy's parole hearing, he told them that Muncie was talking to him about the victim who testified against him at his trial, and that he said, 'I should've taken the bitch's eyes out before she saw me.' "This other convict knew that years earlier a vic' was found without her eyes. Thought he was throwing them a bone."

"Where's Muncie now?" Vin asked.

"Nobody knows. He finished his sentence, no parole. But he's around somewhere. He's from here, with nowhere to go."

Vin asked for and received a picture of Muncie from Turpin's briefcase. He thanked the reporter, and Turpin told him to call him anytime. "I like this guy for this. It sounds right," he said as Vin got up to leave.

17

FROM HARRAH'S, VIN walked east across the French Quarter along St. Peter street, not knowing where it would lead him but needing the time to process the information he was just given.

It was August, and the stifling humidity carried with it the day smells of the Quarter; fresh shrimp and oysters being off-loaded from trucks into the restaurants, the ever present scent of mildew mixing in. He hardly noticed.

Vin was new to the hunter game, and too late realized that he failed to ask the most elementary questions, such as: What was the name of the lead detective on the murders? What were Muncie's vices—did he drink, use drugs, frequent clubs? What was the other inmate's name? More questions were popping up than answers.

He sorely missed Esteen and Miss Jovetta's wisdom, and made an effort to do them justice by taking each element of what he'd learned so far and dissecting it with his elder mentor's logic, and the ancient woman's way of getting into the mind of the person.

The narrow sidewalks were jammed with tourists and locals and maneuvering around them was breaking his concentration. He crossed Bourbon, past the noise of the clubs, and spotted a barber shop on the corner at Royal Street. The shop was empty, and the barber led him immediately to a chair.

"How would you like it?"

"Short."

The barber smiled at the prospect of shearing this shaggy young subject, and swiftly began to cut away, not making an effort at small talk. Losing the weight of hair seemed to clear Vin's mind, and he used the time to formulate a plan of action and come to some logical deductions.

Lost in thought, he was surprised when, in just a few minutes, the barber said, "There ya go!" Vin looked up in the mirror to see himself five years older. High and tight on the sides, with just enough left on top for a center part, he was pleased with what he saw. Respectable and mature came to mind. He paid for the cut, left a five-dollar tip, and walked out onto the street with a confident stride.

Vin walked a block to the next corner, turned

right, and saw something that had a twofold impact on him. He saw an alley. It struck him just then that there had been no alleys in his roaming of the Quarter. This was the only one. All buildings on each block shared an inner court.

It was Pirates Alley. The site of the last "eyes" murders, as he'd come to think of them. The alley was about half a block long, and poured out into Jackson Square, which was teaming with people.

Vin walked the alley to the square, turned and slowly walked it back to the street. "Why here?" he wondered. It was one of five ways to leave the square. The victim was raped and stabbed repeatedly, and her eyes were taken. Somebody must have seen or heard something. What time did the crime take place? Had to have been around four or five a.m. not to have been noticed, and even then, it had to be quick. Not here, he thought. It was done somewhere else, and the body was brought here. That piece of information wouldn't have made it to the public.

Vin sat on a bench next to one of the many street artists, dug out his new cell phone, called Jacob Turpin and asked for the name of the lead detective on the case.

"Liam Nation. A hard man to get ahold of," Turpin said before he hung up.

"Wait! . . . Shit," Vin said to the dial tone.

He had other questions for the reporter but decided not to call him back right away. He didn't want to bother him more this morning. Some people had a life.

Vin got up and followed the square around, looking at artists perched side-by-side doing everything from landscapes to caricatures of the tourists.

He crossed the street and ducked into the Cafe Du Monde. Located between the Mississippi River and the square, the cafe offered the option of indoor or patio dining. The hostess told him that on the patio was a perfect spot for people watching to one side, and you could see the river boats come in on the other. He took an indoor table in a corner and ordered coffee and the only other item on the menu-beignets. Beignets, he was told, were a light pastry covered in powdered sugar, and that they were 'to die for.'

Vin called the New Orleans Police Department and asked for detective Nation. The clerk transferred his call to Nation's voice mail. He left a short message, his name and number, and hung up.

He dug through a building wad of papers in his pocket, looking for Sophie's phone number, finally found it and called her. Her number went straight to voicemail, so he left her his number and asked her to give his regards to the family. Apparently, she had a life too.

His coffee came, with the 'to die for' pastries. They were every bit as good as advertised. When the plate was empty, he looked at his lap and saw that only a fraction of the powdered sugar had made it to his mouth.

Turpin had given Vin a manila folder when he'd asked for a picture of Muncie at the casino. He wet a napkin in his ice-water, cleaned his fingers, and opened the folder. In it, was a full-color eight by ten mug shot. At the bottom were the words, PRE-RE-LEASE. The face looking back at him was worn. Aldo Muncie had jet-black short-cropped hair, and hard dark brown eyes. Along with that was a smaller black and white mug shot, dated thirteen years earlier. In the black and white photo, a much younger Muncie looked back at him. In this picture, he had the look of a trapped animal. The information placard that he was holding under his chin stated: D.O.B. 1-14-77 Incarcerated: 8-3-94. He was 17, Vin noted, and he looked familiar! In a rush, Vin's almost perfect memory brought him back to Pig-Eyes 'art collection.' The photo on the dash, nearest to the passenger seat, was of the boy looking back at him in the mug shot. In the car, the boy in the photo was a little younger, but Vin was sure that this was the same person in the mug shot.

Subconsciously, Vin had always assumed that the

kids in those pictures were dead. But this one got away. The color photo was of a thirty-year-old convict. Vin wanted this image etched into his mind, the image of a monster, but Muncie as a boy kept overriding his attempts to demonize this man. This freak assaulted and raped a woman who survived and testified against him. He was definitely bad news, and the most likely suspect in the case of Camille's murder, and that of the woman in the alley. But he was seventeen when he did the assault. He was a victim of Pig Eyes.

"Damn it!" Vin said. He sipped his coffee, stared at nothing for a moment. "Shit!" he said louder.

A couple at a table not far from him looked up nervously and stared at him. He caught their eyes, and they quickly looked down at their beignets.

He got up then, threw a ten on the table, walked out into the daylight and shuffled toward the boardwalk on the Mississippi. Twice he bumped into pedestrians, mumbled his apologies, and moments later found a bench on the Moon Walk. After a few minutes of watching people depart and others board the Natchez riverboat, he dialed Sophie's number again.

18

VIN'S PHONE WAS ringing. He had been punching in the numbers for Sophie, but he had a call coming in. Unused to cell phones, he didn't know what to do. A number flashed on his screen as it continued to ring. Where were the numbers he just punched in? Irritated, he answered, "What?"

"What do ya mean, what?" an unfamiliar voice said, and continued, "You called me first!"

Vin was perplexed.

"What? I'm sorry. Who is this?"

"Nation. Detective Nation. You called."

"Oh! Yes. Yes, I'm sorry . . . um. I was dialing a number and . . ."

Laughter from the other end, then, "New phone, I bet. Not used to it, huh?"

Vin got his groove back and said, "Yes, Detective Nation, thanks for getting back to me. My name is Ca . . ." He paused and corrected himself. "Vin Robineux."

A chuckle came from the other end, then, "I know."

"Well, I was calling about the Camille . . ." Vin started.

"YEAH, YEAH. I recognize the name. Go on," Nation said. A hint of irritation rising in his voice.

Vin went on, "OK. Well. I talked to Jacob Turpin today, the Times reporter? And he told me about Aldo Muncie . . ."

"Muncie only did this last one," Nation cut him off.

"What?" Vin said.

"He only did this last one," Nation repeated. "He definitely didn't do Camille Robineux. Listen, Vin . . ." The detective paused, "I talked to Sophie a while ago, and she said you're her brother, but not. I was on the Robineux murder investigation, did my interviews, and I know she didn't have a brother. I also know that the Cajun folks will adopt anyone as family, if the spirit moves them." He said this respectfully, as though he admired the sentiment.

"I'm going to tell you this, only because I know and trust Miss Robineux." He paused a moment then went on. "Both of the victims were raped, but the freak used a condom in the second one. There was no trace evidence. With Camille Robineux, we had a semen sample. Just couldn't match it to anyone. Her killer has never been in the system, otherwise we'd have some DNA to use, they all gotta give DNA nowadays. Okay, look, Vin. I don't want to do this over this phone. Let me look at my . . ." He paused then and Vin waited, impatient to ask questions.

"Okay, still there?" Nation said.

"Yes, Sir."

"You know Buster's?" the detective asked.

"Yes. First place I ate when I got here." Vin said.

"Good, meet me there in twenty minutes."

Vin's phone went dead.

He left the Mississippi behind and made his way across the Quarter again. Buster's was only six blocks away, his beignets were wearing off, and he wanted to get there before Nation and have a chance to order before they got down to business.

When he arrived, there was a squad car double-parked in front of the restaurant. He pushed through the saloon-style double doors and saw two uniformed cops standing by the cash register. Vin walked up to them, turned to one of them and asked if they might know where Detective Nation was. The officer behind him, a big man with Italian features and a nose that had seen a few fights, put a hand on his shoulder and attempted to turn him around. Instinct and training overrode Vin's common sense, as he grabbed the hand on his shoulder, bent his knees a little, spun around and turned the hand upside-down and cranked up on it. The cop let out a loud grunt as his knees folded to ease the pain of Vin's Kai hold. It had the opposite effect, and the cop shot up to the tips of his toes, unable to form a word as the pain intensified.

The other officer, a much shorter young black man, immediately drew his Taser, and squeezed the trigger. Four electrically charged barbed wires shot into Vin's lightweight shirt, and the extreme voltage immediately threw him back and to the floor. His grip on the big cop's hand never released but increased due to the muscle-shock. Both men went to the floor, the officer landing hard on Vin's chest.

The smaller cop wedged in between them, threw his partner off, and flipped Vin over, cuffing him while keeping a brutal knee in his neck.

"What the . . . ?!" Vin cried out.

"Not a fuckin' word, dipshit," the big cop said from somewhere behind him. The arresting officer brought him to his feet, threw him against the wall, and began reciting his rights to him. From the corner of his eye, Vin could see a 9mm. semi-auto, held three feet away, and aimed directly at his head.

"Do you understand these rights?" the little cop asked through clenched teeth.

"Yes." Vin was calm now. He slowed his breathing with effort.

"Nation just wanted us to bring you in. Check you out," Bent-Nose said. "Now you done pissed me off, boy."

The big cop opened the door and punched Vin in the kidney as he said, "Get in! Quit resisting!"

Vin collapsed head-first across the seat as someone slammed the door hard into the bottom of his feet.

"BECAUSE YOU'RE A ghost," Detective Nation said, when Vin asked about the criminal treatment he received on his way to the station.

Nation was standing off to the side as a booking officer was guiding Vin's fingers through ink then rolling them on a fingerprint card. The NOPD lost their state-of-the-art fingerprint scanning system during Katrina and were making do with the old-school methods.

"You're lucky I don't lock you up until we can verify who you are. Sophie Robineux may trust you, but I can't. You came into her life out of nowhere."

"As a favor to her," he went on, "I've convinced the uniforms not to press charges on you for assault and resisting arrest."

Vin started to respond to this but caught himself. Instead, he took the opportunity to size up the detective; Tall, lean, broad-shouldered and obviously Native American.

The booking officer signaled that he was finished, and Nation led Vin to his office. The small room smelled of mildew, but it was clean. Water damage was evident near the baseboards and the only window was boarded up.

"Hurricane did it," Nation said, as he followed Vin's eyes. "I got lucky, didn't have an office before the big blow, but now the force is down to a third, and there's room for everyone!"

Vin waited. Besides Sophie, he hadn't met many people as talkative as the detective.

"Have you got a cigarette?" Vin asked.

Nation smiled and said, "Only in the movies, Kid. No-one smokes in public buildings anymore."

The 'ghost' went silent again. This cop had offered up some information over the phone earlier, but now Vin was second-guessing himself on whether this was friend or foe sitting before him. Nothing, he realized more and more, was as it seems. Nobody was an ally. He had no friends here. He missed Esteen's company.

"I know that look, son." Nation continued, "OK. Here's the score. You said your last name was Robineux. I know that's not true. No tattoo tells me I'm probably not going to find you in the system." The detective paused, reached in his desk drawer, and pulled out a pack of cigarettes. Nodding toward the pack, he said, "I lied." He swiveled his chair, grabbed a loose board from the window to ventilate the room, and shook out a smoke for Vin.

They both walked over to the window and lit up, and Nation went on. "This is the new-New Orleans. If a warrant doesn't come up for you, I don't care who you are . . ." He stopped, faced Vin and said. "I want to help you. Muncie is the wrong guy for Camille's murder, but I like him for this last one. You're on the street, closer to things than I am. Muncie just got out, no family, and nowhere to go. He's here . . . somewhere, and you'll probably find him before I do. He didn't kill Camille, but he knows who did. He's a copycat killer, he knows who the original is, now we gotta find them both."

At the word 'we,' Vin raised his eyebrows. Nation was alright. Maybe.

19

VIN WAS FREE to go. On his way out of the House of Detention, Nation reminded him that what they discussed was a police matter, so if he found Aldo Muncie, just call 911. A little wiser now, Vin didn't say what was on his mind.

Walking down Carondelet Street, the Quarter drew him back like a magnet. He set his mental compass for that heading and dialed Sophie's number on the way.

"Calvin! I'm so glad you called!" Sophie answered on the first ring. Vin sensed distress in her voice and let her go on.

"Uncle is gone. He got a call on my cell from that reporter and, without a word, left quickly in his Jeep. He hasn't been himself ever since the anniversary of Mother's murder."

Her voice was cracking, and Vin was taken aback. She was more prone to anger than anguish.

He let a long moment pass, collecting his thoughts as he crossed Canal Street, and finally said, "I don't know what Turpin said to him, but I bet Esteen's headed this way. I'll call Turpin right away and find out. Okay?"

"Okay. Yes please, do that. Memaw is worried. Daddy wouldn't have left her in her condition for anything less than an emergency. At first, I thought something had happened to you, but then I know that the police or hospital would have called." She choked back a sob then, and said, "Call me, Cousin. I don't like what I'm feeling."

"I will. OK? I will." He hung-up.

Vin stopped by a Lucky Dog vendor on the corner of Bourbon and Toulouse and dialed Turpin's number while telling the vendor that he wanted a foot long. While the phone rang, he watched his grayish-pink lunch being prepared, and groaned with hunger and disgust. Jacob Turpin's voicemail kicked in on the fourth ring, and Vin left a message for him to call back as soon as possible.

With all the condiments available, he created a culinary camouflage covering over his meal, ordered a soda, and sat on nearby steps which led to someone's home. Vin was having his first French Quarter picnic.

He called Sophie, and with a mouth full of food, told her that he would try Turpin again. ". . . and Sophie, just call me Vin from now on. OK?"

"Sure, Calvin. Whatever. Call me back soon."

Vin was relieved to hear her a little back to normal.

Finished with the assault on his palate, he brought his trash over to the dog-stand's trash bag and gave the vendor a $5 'pity' tip. The Lucky Dog slinger smiled weakly, knowing the gesture for what it was.

It was late afternoon, and Bourbon was filling up early with revelers anticipating the night. Wanting to get away from the growing crowd, Vin walked a block to Johnny White's.

Jimmy, the slow learning bartender from the night before, wasn't behind the bar this time. A younger, muscular, tattooed biker type was lazily quenching the thirst of the few professional drinkers. Some of the faces Vin recognized from the night before, but Sheree the Hooker was nowhere to be seen. No loss.

Vin ordered a rum and coke, made his way to a dark corner booth, and went over what he knew about the case so far. The case. He realized that that is what he came to think of his mission. Who did he think he was, anyway? Barely an adult, at an age where you could drink only in Louisiana and trying to find a murderer. This was about family, about what was important to them and he liked it. Like he was born to the hunt.

Aldo Muncie may not have killed Camille, may not have done this last murder, but he knew who did. Vin knew it, sensed it more than anything. Muncie made the eyes comment to his old cellmate. Where did that come from? Nation didn't really think Muncie did this last one, Vin could see it in the detective's eyes. But Nation knew the ex-con was the key.

20

JOHNNY WHITE'S WAS getting crowded. He wasn't up to it. A three-block walk brought him back to Jackson Square. The sun was setting, some of the artists were packing up for the day and the night tribe of street people appeared out of the shadows. He picked a bench facing Pirates Alley and began to unpack the folder of information that Turpin had provided. He had half of the contents around him on the bench when his cell phone rang.

When he answered, Jacob Turpin told him that he couldn't imagine what he might have said to Esteen to get him to leave the house. Turpin also gave Vin the name of the Pirates Alley victim; Lelani Barden. She was, Turpin had just discovered, Aldo Muncie's fiancée before he'd been busted.

"Wow, huh?" Turpin said. "Who would've figured? I talked to Muncie's old cellmate Jonas Dellenbaugh. He said that girl had Muncie's heart. No way had he killed her. Now I'm thinking that trail is cold."

"Did you tell Esteen about her?"

"No, he told ME. That's why I called the cellmate. To get some background."

"Who told Esteen?"

"Nation, I guess," Turpin said. "Good luck, gotta go, Ok?" Then the reporter hung up.

Esteen knew about Lelani Barden? Vin called Liam Nation. It was late, and the extension went to voicemail. Frustrated, Vin left a call-me-back message.

Fire eaters, musicians, jugglers and tourists were now mingling in the square. Street people, an expected part of the ambiance, were weaving among the masses looking for the sick and the weak among the herd.

Lost in thought, photos and clippings surrounding him, Vin didn't notice the underage bohemian girl sit down next to him on the only empty spot left.

"Aldo! Is that a mug shot? That's sooo cool!" she said.

Vin's head jerked up.

"What?!"

"That's Aldo. Are you writing a book about him or something? I mean, he's like a so cool guy. Oh my god, that would be the shit!"

"You know him?" Vin said. His hands began to tremble.

"Yeah. Hey, you're like shaking and stuff." Her eyes narrowed. "Wait. You're like a reporter or a cop, huh?" She got up then, turned, and Vin caught her wrist.

"HEY! Motherfucker! Let go of me right NOW!" She said it loud enough to get people's heads to turn. He couldn't let go. Had to keep her longer.

"Stop," he said calmly. "I'll give you twenty dollars to sit down."

A big Viking-looking street dweller was approaching fast from the left, and she waved him off. Behind the big man was a 140-pound hollow-eyed rat face following close behind.

"You sure you're OK, Night Eyes?" Rat face said.

"Yeah guys. I got this," she said, grinning at Vin as she sat back down. "These guys would kill for me, you know?" she beamed. The two street skells walked slowly backwards, giving Vin what they thought was a hard look before finally turning around and disappearing into the crowd.

When he was still Calvin, before the Robineuxs, Vin had been wandering aimlessly around the country. He did day labor jobs, washed dishes, and even panhandled a little to get by. At nights he slept outside. In the city that meant sleeping in parks, under bridges, or abandoned warehouses.

He was always among and around the street tribe, but never one of them. Never in town long enough to be trusted; he found himself on the perimeter. Watching.

In the seven short months before he came to Louisiana, he had seen a lot of girls like the one before him.

These guys were not her friends; they were predators. Patient, waiting for the right time and place they would feed her, keep her warm and dry, and turn her into a money-making machine. She was fresh-faced, probably from good stock, just out for an adventure. Couldn't be more than 15.

"Night Eyes, is it?"

"Um . . . yeah." She unconsciously untied the tie-dyed T-shirt that exposed her flat belly and smoothed it out.

Vin reached in his pocket, extracted a hundred from his roll, and gave it to her. Her eyes went wide as she took it, and Vin recognized the fear.

"Listen. I just want to talk. Really." He could see then that she was not as fresh as he'd first thought. But not ruined. Yet.

"I AM writing a book about Aldo, okay? I was hoping to catch up to him when he got out of Angola, but I had the dates screwed up." He gave her a sly smile, and went on, "Shhh. Big secret, OK? This guy, you have no idea. He's a piece of work. Reformed ex-con, trying to integrate back into society, misunderstood. He's charming, witty, and the world won't give him a chance. I want to BE that chance! But I need your help." Beignets, hotdogs, and alcohol were rising to his esophagus as he finished spewing out more lies than he thought he was capable of. He was changing, and he was losing himself in the process.

His charismatic explanation, along with his boyish good looks, set the girl at ease.

She smiled big then and said, "You DO understand him! Aldo is cooler than the others. He doesn't come around much, you know? He mostly stays under the I-10 overpass at Elysian Fields. He's a writer too, you know? He like, just writes all day and comes around the square sometimes at night." Night Eyes got up then, said "Bye!" and walked off quickly in the same direction as her protectors.

21

ALDO MUNCIE WAITED. He didn't mind waiting; thirteen years in prison taught him patience. He saw the taxi slow to a stop a block away. Most of the streetlights were still damaged from the hurricane, so he couldn't see the passenger's face when he got out, but he knew it was him. Night Eyes had done her job.

Aldo was sick of running, hiding. He'd done his time. Jake told him someone was coming around asking questions. Jake was one of Master Benny's boys too. Aldo had escaped from his pig-eyed captor by working the nails out of the boards of the shed where he and the others had been held; Jacob Turpin would work one side and Aldo the other. They'd used their spoons to pry out the nails. The other kids had been there too long, their spirits crushed by the cigar chomping freak's frequent visits. As the two boys worked, the others just looked on.

Jake and Aldo escaped together that night. They traveled together until at daylight they had found a forked road. They agreed that getting picked-up would be easier if they split up. Jake would go south, Aldo north. Before they parted, they made a pact that neither of them would go to the police.

Jacob had come from a wealthy family, and the embarrassment of what Master Benny had done to him would be more than he could bear, more scandal than his politician father could overcome. He would just say he ran away, and that he had come home because it was too tough being away.

Aldo had been passed from one abusive foster family to another, until eventually he had just run away. He didn't want to go back.

SMILIN' CHRIS PULLED away from the curb, and Vin quickly made his way behind a tree. He looked under the dark overpass but couldn't see anyone in the shadows. Crouching low he advanced from bush to tree, crossing people's yards. He took his time, not wanting to alert his prey. Esteen's sorrow and Sophie's anger were his motivators. For the sake of his new family, Vin proceeded with caution. If Muncie was up there, he would not kill him. Liam Nation was right; this was a police matter. But Vin had picked up a mini-recorder on the way to the overpass. He wanted Aldo Muncie to confess to Camille's murder. Even if he had to beat it out of him.

As Vin approached the forty-five-degree slope, Aldo lit a cigarette, exposing his position. Vin knew that he'd been seen, so he charged up the slope hoping to catch Muncie before he got away. Halfway up Vin heard a metallic click and froze in his tracks.

22

"I DIDN'T DO anything," Muncie said, from somewhere in the darkness. He was on the move since he'd lit his cigarette.

Vin reached for the lighter-sized mini-recorder to free it from his pants pocket.

Don't," Muncie said, again from another location.

"Keep 'em where I can see 'em and walk up here. Don't play with me or I'll end you."

"I'm not armed," Vin said, as he scuffed his way slowly up the incline. He reached the top, ducking under the overpass I-beams. A hand reached out to his collar and pulled him into the cramped space. Vin let it happen.

Muncie inhaled on his cigarette, illuminating Vin as the ex-con patted him down. He paused at the recorder, and again at Vin's phone, and went on. When he was finished, he scuttled out of reach.

"You roll up on me with no piece? I oughta shoot the stupid out of you," Muncie hissed. "Jake said you was comin'. Said you took out his boy at the motel like you was Karate Man. I ain't that easy."

"That thug at the motel? Jake? Who's Jake?" Vin said a little loudly, hoping the voice-activated recorder was picking up the conversation.

Muncie, still aiming his gun from his lap, reached over and turned on a battery powered low-light camping lamp.

Vin took in his surroundings in a glance. They were seated on a three-foot concrete ledge. Muncie was sitting on a sleeping bag, surrounded by a notebook, Walkman, cigarettes, and a throw-away cellphone much like Vin's.

"Rich boy Turpin said you weren't too bright. Out of your league, he said." Muncie chuckled and re-lit his cigarette left-handed, careful not to let his gun-hand waver.

"Turpin," Vin mumbled. Absorbing what he was hearing. Thinking it through. Think, then do.

Aldo Muncie slid one of his notebooks towards Vin and said, "Not in a hurry are ya? Read chapter one of my guaranteed money-maker sad piss-poor life story."

"I don't want . . ."

"Fuck what you want, Bitch! You look at that shit

and tell me if you think I did a *damn* thing. I sure didn't kill anybody."

Vin looked into the eyes of the shell of a man across from him. Muncie was angry, pathetic, hard but not evil. Vin had danced with the devil before, and this felt different. He asked Aldo for a smoke, had a lit one tossed to him, and began reading.

THE WRITING WAS in pencil at first, the penmanship terrible. He read about how Master Benny had kidnapped Muncie as a teenager while he was hitchhiking. Vin's vision temporarily blurred as he mentally replayed his own encounter with the pig-eyed freak.

Muncie had met Turpin in a locked shed occupied by two other boys and a girl. Jacob Turpin had been snatched from a mall just two days earlier. At the mention of Turpin, Muncie stated that he didn't like or trust him, but he at least had the balls to help him escape.

Aldo spent a week there. Watching as their captor picked a different kid every couple hours and dragged them outside kicking and screaming. Once, when Muncie tried to bolt through the open door, the big man punched him hard in the temple, sending him to his knees vomiting.

Two days before the escape, the only girl in the shed sat next to Aldo. She said her name was Lelani Barden, had been there a month, and that she was thirteen. They leaned against the wall and talked about what they missed on the outside, and Lelani said she missed the way she felt when she looked into her mother's loving eyes. Master Benny growled from the other side of the wall then.

The door opened a moment later and the pig-eyed freak crooked his finger at Lelani. She stood and peed herself as she approached the big man. When she got close, he leaned down and said around his cigar, "What color were mommy's eyes?" She told him, and he turned and walked away, slamming the door behind him and engaging the lock from the outside.

Master Benny returned the next day. When he opened the door, he rolled a mason jar filled with liquid at Lelani's feet and said, "You're my favorite toy, so I brought you something. I'll let you thank me in that special way tonight." Pig-eyes growled at her, chuckled, and went out the door.

Aldo rolled the jar with his foot then, and two blue eyes floated to the surface. Lelani screamed then, screamed and screamed and then scurried to a dark corner, rolled into a fetal position, and moaned until Master Benny came for her hours later.

EACH DAY THAT Muncie had written about had the date as a header. The day Master Benny brought Lelani her gift was labeled; August 3, 1994. The day Camille lost her eyes.

23

"SO YOU KNOW," Vin said as he set the notebook down, "Turpin put me on to you."

Aldo Muncie lowered the pistol to his lap. He kept his grip on it, but let the barrel aim towards the ground as he said, "Yeah. I'm startin' to put that together . . ." He let the words trail away.

Vin saw the gun lower, and relaxed a bit and said, "He also told my Uncle, who was the husband of the woman who died for the eyes that were in that jar, about the comment you made to your old cellmate about taking the eyes of the woman who testified against you . . ."

"I never said that shit!" Muncie's voice rose along with the barrel of his gun. "That ol' boy was just trying to score points with the parole board. I never assaulted that woman either, that was a set-up!" The ex-con made a forlorn noise. It sounded to Vin like the sound a wounded animal makes.

"And so your Uncle came down to the Quarter and killed Lelani! How did he know that she was all I had left in this world?!" Muncie moaned, his gun hand shaking.

Vin sat in stunned silence. Aldo Muncie made a gurgling sound and Vin looked up in time to see the gunman topple over, an arrow sticking out of his neck. Muncie released his grip on the pistol and it began to slide down the incline, as he reached for the shaft ticking out of his neck. He was on his back now, the whites of his eyes showing large as his feet started to rap out a beat on the concrete.

Vin leapt across the distance between them, covering the convulsing man and searching frantically for something, anything, that he could use to stem the blood that was shooting out of the neck wound.

He grabbed Muncie's shirt, ripped a large swath from it, and packed it around the arrow. Vin looked left, right and across the street in search of the shooter, while trying to calm the gunman who had now become his patient.

"Calvin! Is he dead, cher?" Esteen's voice came from the darkness across the street.

"No, wounded, but I need help."

THE STEEL-EYED CAJUN, his bow slung over his

shoulder, arrived at the top of the incline as Vin was wrapping the shivering Muncie in a sleeping bag. Esteen leaned in to help bring the wounded man down the incline and a block away to where he had parked the Jeep. No one walked or drove by as they loaded the man into the vehicle. This was the edge of the hurricane torn Ninth Ward. The few homes that remained were mostly deserted and far apart from each other.

Vin's motel room was just a mile from Charity Hospital; he had passed it a few times, so he knew how to guide the older man to the emergency room. Muncie was unconscious but alive. As they made their way across town, Esteen told Vin to snap off both ends of the arrow, but not to pull it out lest the man bled to death. Vin did this, and then used what was left of the victim's shirt to pack both sides of the wound.

At the Ambulance Only entrance to the emergency room, both men off-loaded the wounded man, rushed him through the door and onto a bed that was already being rushed toward them by hospital staff.

Both men were led away to the ER waiting room, where Vin made a call to Liam Nation. As he explained the situation over the phone, a hospital security guard was talking Esteen out of his bow, with some difficulty.

24

THE MURDER RATE was up in New Orleans and Charity Hospital's ER was buzzing. Distressed, angry, and sick were all represented in the crowded lobby.

Only two seats remained that were side-by-side, and Vin and Esteen were in them, discussing murder. No one cared or noticed.

The elder man listened as Vin repeated his conversation with Muncie. When the story got to the part about the ex-con's memoirs, and Muncie's assumption that Vin's father had killed Lelani Barden, Esteen only shook his head. "I know it wasn't you," Vin assured him.

"So. Jacob Turpin . . . I'm not sure I understand how . . ." Esteen started.

"What about Turpin?" Liam Nation said, suddenly appearing by their side.

Both men looked up suddenly at the voice.

"Uncle, this is Detective Nation," Vin said.

"Oui. We've met."

"You know each other?"

"Sure. Mr. Robineux was a frequent visitor to the station, back when I was still in uniform," Nation said as he reached down to shake Esteen's rough, brown hand.

"Hoo-wee! He's still got a grip too!" Nation said through a wince.

The detective nodded toward the exit and said, "Let's go outside and talk, this place is depressing."

All three men headed toward the door, Esteen pausing long enough to retrieve his bow and quiver from the security station. He caught up as they were going through the door and Nation nodded at the bow and said, "I'm going to need to hold that for evidence."

Esteen looked at Vin, who nodded reassuringly, and turned over the bow and quiver reluctantly. Nation thanked him, understanding a man's bond with his weapons, and tossed both into the trunk of his unmarked sedan parked near the entrance.

THEY FOLLOWED AS the detective approached a set of benches, one of which seemed to be occupied by a pile of old clothing and newspapers. The pile sat straight up when Nation kicked the iron arm rest. Large, bloodshot eyes looked defiantly out at the men from beneath a nest of hair and a grease colored ball cap which read "81st. Airborne Rangers."

Nation said nothing, giving the man his five second cop's stare. The old veteran mumbled something, gathered his pile, shambled off through some bushes and disappeared silently into the darkness, like he was trained to do decades ago.

The homicide detective, sitting on the recently vacated bench, listened and took notes on a small pad as Vin, sitting on the nearby bench with his father, told the detective everything he had learned in his meeting with Muncie. Esteen said nothing but listened intently as he rolled cigarettes, handing a lit one to his son.

When Vin had finished, Nation said, "So. Esteen thought that you were in mortal danger, and did what he did to save you." It wasn't a question, but a summation of the facts. The detective lit his own cigarette and said nothing for a full minute.

Each man sat silently, staring out at the traffic on Tulane Avenue, processing the information.

25

NATION LED THE other two men back into the hospital and into the intensive care unit where Aldo Muncie was being treated.

The charge nurse answered in the affirmative when Nation asked if Muncie was conscious, and all three men filed into the patient's room.

Muncie tracked them with his eyes as they made a semi-circle around his bed. His neck was dressed with large gauze bandages over the entrance and exit wounds. A clear plastic wrap circled his neck and held the dressing in place. Above and to his left were a bag of saline, and a liquid painkiller which were attached to an I.V. in his arm.

"Not a friend in the room," Muncie said as he looked around. "Kinda like being back in the joint."

"Been a while," Nation said.

"Yeah. I didn't miss you. Almost didn't recognize you, Nation. No uniform. No fresh rosy rookie cheeks. What are ya'? Some kinda big-shot detective now?"

"Something like that," Nation said. "Listen. These two men? They're not your enemies . . ."

"What?! I ain't got many friends, but ain''t none of them shot me with no arrow before. That old motherfuc . . ."

"Was defending his nephew," the detective said, cutting him off. "You did have a gun on him."

Nodding towards Vin, Muncie said, "He was rolling up on my camp! A man don't roll up on a convict quiet like that 'less he's looking to take him out."

Vin started to open his mouth when Nation held up his hand and shook his head.

"Whatever, Muncie," the cop said. "Fact is, you're an ex-con in possession of a firearm. You're looking at five years for a dumbshit move like that. I can make that charge go away . . . if you don't press charges against Mr. Robineux here."

Muncie shook his head violently and grimaced as he aggravated his wound, said, "Jake told me that old dude killed Lelani! Freak son-of-a-bitch took her eyes out! And shoots me in the neck . . ."

"Turpin told you? That Esteen killed her?" Nation said.

"Yeah," Muncie said through gritted teeth, as he

pushed the button in his hand which released the painkiller into his I.V.

"All right. You two guys grab a chair. The four of us, we're gonna have a meeting," Nation said.

Vin and Esteen each grabbed the only two available chairs in the room, scooted them toward the bed, and sat down. Liam Nation pushed Muncie's legs over and took a spot on the end of the bed.

Nodding to Esteen, Nation said, "Sir. Jacob Turpin used you to get to Muncie. I'm sure of it." Nodding at Vin, he went on, "He put you onto Muncie's trail too. I think he was trying to increase his chances that, between the two of you, one of you would get to Muncie and kill him."

Looking over at Aldo Muncie, the detective went on, "Turpin told you that Esteen killed Lelani. Right? And he probably hooked you up with that gun. Told you someone was coming for you." Muncie said nothing, but nodded his head.

Nation paused then, putting it all together in his head before he went on.

Vin broke the silence and said to Muncie, "I thought you last saw Lelani back at that shed. How did you get in a relationship with her?"

Muncie pushed himself up on the bed, tapped out a dose of painkiller with his button. "Ol' Master Benny didn't kill the kids when he was done with them.

I found this out when I saw Lelani in the Quarter a couple weeks after I escaped. We were all blindfolded when he brought us there, and Lelani said that when he got bored with a kid, he would pack them back in the car again, blindfolded, drive for hours and push them out."

Aldo was not looking at anyone as he spoke, but at some point over their heads as he went on, "Lelani and I found each other. She was too ashamed to go back to her parents; I didn't have no-one. So, we survived together. Did whatever dark shit we had to, to get by. I think I loved her . . . she said she loved me. Then I caught this bullshit assault charge and never saw her again."

Exhausted, he relaxed and closed his eyes and said. "I'm fried. Can't talk no more, this painkiller's getting me messed up."

"Mr. Robineux is off the hook, right?" Nation said, letting the ice show in his voice.

"Yeah," Muncie mumbled. A tear leaked from one of his closed eyes and tracked a trail down his dirty cheek.

"Just a few more loose ends, gentlemen," Nation said as he got up. "Let's take this back outside and let this guy rest."

26

OUTSIDE THE HOSPITAL entrance, Nation popped his trunk and returned the bow and quiver to the quiet bayou man with the steel-colored eyes.

"Merci. For everything," Esteen said.

"No. Thank you, Mr. Robineux. I do believe you could have taken the kill shot . . . but you didn't. Saved me a lot of paperwork."

Esteen only nodded.

From the nearby bench, the glow of a cigarette could be seen from just inside the pile of clothes and papers that had returned to its roost. Following suit, each man standing around the unmarked sedan lit one of his own.

After a few moments, Nation said, "Turpin's father is a well-respected and well-connected Orleans Parish commissioner. He's expected to run, and win, in the next mayoral race." Aiming his cigarette at

Vin, he went on. "From what you told me earlier, I'm guessing Jacob Turpin is methodically trying to take down everyone who might connect him to having been abducted or having known the killer of Camille Robineux. He has pitted all interested parties against each other without having raised a finger . . ."

Vin spoke up then, "What about Lelani Barden? He killed . . ."

"We can't prove that. Yet."

At that moment, Vin heard Miss Jovetta's voice in his head, "Calvin!" The gator/snake ring on his finger glowed lightly. Esteen and Vin saw it.

"Sophie!" Esteen hissed, and immediately turned towards his Jeep. Vin's phone rang then, and he answered it on the run, close on the heels of his uncle. From behind them, the confused detective said, "Hey! What?" But neither Robineux heard him.

Esteen threw the Jeep into gear. Vin on the seat next to him was talking into a silent cell-phone, "Say something! Sophie? Tell me what . . ."

"She can't come to the phone right now," Jacob Turpin said. Vin barely recognized the voice of the man he had only talked to a couple of times. This voice was breathless, unsteady. More silence.

"You piece of shit motherfuc . . ." Vin started to say as the click and dial tone met his ear.

Esteen jumped the landscaping in the circular

drive of the hospital and shifted down as they tore up sod across the hospital grounds. They jumped the curb onto the street, hitting Tulane Avenue in fourth gear.

27

SOPHIE REGAINED CONSCIOUSNESS on the floor of the foyer, in a pool of blood that was congealing beneath her head, causing it to stick to the cold marble. The searing pain caused her to vomit. The act of getting sick made her head feel like it was going to crack open.

The stun gun that Turpin hit her in the neck with lay by a nearby window. He had been fast when she answered the door. Still, she raged at being surprised. A guttural gurgling growl escaped her gritted teeth and echoed loudly around the enormous room. Her hands and feet were bound tightly with nylon cord. Struggling to move, the blinding pain in her head reminded her that she was injured. Badly, maybe. How bad? She tested her vision, straining to look as far as possible left and right. Good.

" 'ophie! You ok, cheri?" Miss Jovetta's alarmed, stroke damaged voice came from the kitchen.

"Hush the fuck up, Hag!" Turpin growled.

He slapped her then. Hard. The sound carried to where Sophie lay.

"You die today!"

The bound martial-arts instructor growled. She hammered her shoulder against the marble floor, dislocating it intentionally to get slack into the cord wrapped around her wrist, and screamed in agony and rage.

She saw the color drain from the killer's face as she sprung forward.

Esteen and Vin crashed through the door just in time to see Sophie land a blow to Turpin's solar plexus. When the killer doubled over in pain, she grabbed his head in both hands and twisted it violently. Everyone in the room heard the neck crack.

28

CHARITY HOSPITAL ALLOWED Sophie and Miss Jovetta to share a room. The elder woman needed stitches on her cheek from the crack across the face from Jacob Turpin. The ER doctor wanted her kept overnight for observation because of her advanced age. Sophie's leg wound missed an artery by two millimeters, but the exit wound tore up enough meat to require three hours of surgery.

Esteen sat with his mother and daughter, while Vin and Detective Liam Nation were two doors down in Aldo Muncie's room. Originally the police and the Robineuxs were focusing on him as their prime suspect in the death of Camille, and of Lelani Barden, but the bitter ex-con was no killer. Vin was explaining how Jacob Turpin had been pitting all parties against each other when Muncie asked, "So why didn't he kill the women before y'all got there?"

"Because," Vin started. "He wanted them alive as bait for my father and me. He told Sophie that he intended to take us all out at once."

Liam Nation added, "He set you up as the killer, hoping the Robineuxs would do his dirty work for him, and kill you. He wanted everyone who knew about his past—his shame—-to be dead."

Aldo Muncie shook his head and winced at the pain in his neck wound. He turned his face towards the window slowly and mumbled, What about Master Benny?"

The detective started to say, "It looks like we'll never . . ." Vin cut him off with a raised hand. Nation raised an eyebrow at the young man and Vin motioned for him to follow him out of the room.

When both men were in the hallway, Nation said, "I don't want to know, do I?"

"No."

"Will I ever?" the detective asked with a wry grin.

"No," Vin said. His face told no tale. His stare was neutral.

"I think I have some paperwork to do. Call me." Liam Nation turned and walked around the corner and out of sight.

Vin walked back into the room and told Muncie a story about a hitchhiker and a freak. When he was done, he handed Muncie a photograph.

"My father found this floating by the crash site."

He handed the injured survivor the polaroid and a lighter.

FURTHER

EDDY COOK

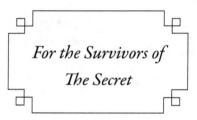

For the Survivors of
The Secret

Part I

Vin

1

"SLACKER, GET UP!"

Chris outside my door. My only friend, and driver. I'm off the grid. When I first rolled into New Orleans, Chris was my first cabbie. He's been getting me where I need to go ever since.

He never knocks, just speaks through the door. I got up from the kitchen table, black coffee in hand, made my way over to the door and snapped the dead bolt open.

"Palaver?" I said.

"Yeah, you right."

Palaver, a word my father uses for a sit down discussion. It was understood that we wouldn't waste words until we both had a cup in one hand and a smoke in the other. I poured a cup for my brother while he lit a smoke. It was 2 pm. I had been up for about fifteen minutes. The ebony, eternally smiling guy across the table from me knew that this was morning for me. We're both night owls but, as far as I know, he never sleeps. That makes me the slacker. Whatever. Asshole. I wake up homicidal. He thinks it's hilarious.

"So. I got a call," he said.

"Money?"

"Don't think so."

"Figures. Moon Bat?"

I look into things for people. Chris has the connections around the city, sets up meetings for me. Sometimes we get some delusional moon-bats asking me to block the all-seeing-eyes that Big Brother uses to track them through their TV's, or to help them prove to the authorities that they had been abducted by aliens and have returned with an important message for humanity. Chris screens my clients.

A few years ago I killed a kid-raping freak in self-defense and tracked down one of his victims that grew into a killer. The word traveled though the underground of the Big Easy that I had the instinct and skills to find people that the law couldn't or wouldn't. Most of the time, somebody was willing to pay. Lately, only the Crazy Tribe has been reaching out to me. I lit my second smoke of the day, emptied my cup, and said, "So?"

"So. A lady called me. Wouldn't say much, except that she needed you to help her hunt."

"Hunt?"

"Hunt. Yeah. Someone's been snatching kids. Three, so far."

Kids. Chris knew I'd deal myself in. I had Chris call the woman back and let her know that I'd be willing to meet with her at Buster's Kitchen at 5:00 that evening. That left a few hours to kill, and Chris had my afternoon planned out for me, wanted me to take a ride with him.

"Big surprise," he said.

I hate surprises. I went anyway. After all, it's not like I had a life or anything. Chris took me on a ten-minute drive from my apartment on the edge of the Quarter to the Ninth Ward. What was left of it.

A few months before I arrived in Louisiana, Hurricane Katrina ripped New Orleans a new asshole. The Ninth Ward was where the levy broke and, even eight years later, the area still had the look and feel of a New Orleans style cemetery. Most of the destroyed homes had been removed, but the trailers that stood in their place looked like above ground tombs. Here and there some ambitious souls were trying to rebuild their lives, but the majority of the displaced families never returned.

Chris drove to the edge of the most deserted

neighborhood, did a U-turn at the end of a long straight street, and killed the engine.

"I never asked you, how did you get to be twenty-six years old and still got no license?"

I reached into the pocket of my lightweight short-sleeved white shirt, brought out my smokes, and lit one from the car lighter. I was stalling. Thinking about how and where to begin. My only friend and I didn't have too many heart to heart conversations when it came to our past. Our relationship was based on mutual respect and some kind of unidentifiable comradery. I decided on the condensed version. I told him a tale that gave a kid a lifetime of sleepless nights. Straight up with the killings.

"Damn," was all Chris could manage. I didn't expect more. He got out of the car then and we switched places. He talked me through the vehicle's operation, and we spent the rest of the afternoon tearing up his cab's transmission.

I GOT TO Buster's at 4:45, ahead of a 5 o'clock meeting, and had the place to myself. The manager, an extra-large black woman everyone called Miss Sheline, was my waitress.

She waved when I came in, grabbed a pot of coffee and waddled her way to my table. She flashed her pearly whites at me as she poured a cup and said, "Somethin' to eat, Vin?"

"No, ma'am."

"Aw, come on now. Fine young man like you, you need your portions! Oh . . . or is it business today?"

"Business."

"A'ight then. Someday I'm gonna give you some business. Mmmm mmm, you have no idea . . ."

He winked and laughed and steamrolled her way back behind the counter. I grinned around a shot of coffee and looked around for a discarded Times-Pic-ayune to read until five. I spotted a paper on a win-dow ledge, walked over to pick it up, and that's when my mystery caller walked through the door. She barely glanced at me as she scanned the room. She was short and plump with close cropped red hair and stylish pink eyeglasses. She looked around again, , frowned and sat in a corner booth. I eased over to my table with the paper under my arm, grabbed my coffee, and stepped up to her booth. She looked me over nervously and said, "Please, don't. I'm meeting someone and I . . ."

"I'm him," I said.

"No. Really, boy. Get away. Shoo. I mean it!"

I get that a lot. I'm cursed with a baby-face, 5'11, dark bangs, and dark eyes. I only need to shave twice a week.

"You called me about kids," I said. Patient.

She lowered her head, looked over her glasses at me and said, "Vin? I'm sorry, I didn't . . ."

"I know. May I join you?"

Her ample cheeks flushed deep scarlet as she nodded. I set my cup down across from her as she lifted a laptop out of her large designer purse and set it in front of me before my coffee's ripples had a chance to smooth out. She looked at me intensely then, saying nothing and holding the computer closed with her hand.

"My name is Fran. The children are all that matter. Do you believe that? I need to know that you do . . ."

"I do." More than she would ever know.

She held my eyes, nodded to herself and opened the laptop. She whispered something about picking up a wireless signal from the bohemian coffee shop across the street and gave me a wink like I was in on the secret. I can barely figure out a cell phone. I winked back like I wasn't the tech-tard that I am. On screen after screen I read articles from various Minnesota newspapers, each with a common thread.

Endangered runaway Corey Maki missing from Eveleth, MN. since 01/12/15, male age 14. After extensive questioning, none of his friends or family seem to know where he might be. Corey's been diagnosed ADD and has had problems with authority in the past. Police believe that foul play is not an issue in this case.

Ashley Hultgren, age 13, missing since 07/16/15 from Britt, MN never returned from a church over-night lock-in. She was last seen the following morn-ing walking the two blocks to her home. Police sus-pect foul play.

Zach Karpinen, age 14, was last seen 04/22/16 when he got separated from his father and the rest of a deer hunting party while roaming the woods near Mt. Iron, MN. Friends, neighbors, and three law en-forcement agencies from surrounding counties have been unable to find any trace of the missing boy.

I LOOKED UP when I was finished and she told me she would text the link to this file to Chris's smart phone. I nodded like I knew what she was talking about. Chris says I'm a Luddite. I've always meant to look that up.

"They were all taken, and we know who took them. It's not one person . . ."

She began talking faster, wringing her hands.

"They had me once for two years, they kept us in locked stalls at a barn but I got away. It was in the papers up north back in the 90's . . ."

"What?" I tried to interrupt, but she cut me off

and went on, "Two of them got caught, I tried to tell anyone who would listen that there were other Trainers but there was no proof. So one of them, Rod Hilde, got 11 years for kidnapping and child molestation, and the other one, Jimmy Tapio, got eight years for aiding and abetting a kidnapping."

I put up a STOP hand and said, "Wait. Trainers?" was all I was able to get out before she started gushing again.

Her voice rose an octave as she went on, but Miss Shaline didn't seem to mind. She understood my work better than most. We came from the same tribe.

"Trainers. That's what they referred to themselves as. I was being groomed as a sex slave for a group that dealt in selling and trading as a lifestyle—not for profit as much as they just enjoyed it. I met other kids held by other trainers, but only at secret places that I would never be able to find again because of the blindfold."

She paused then and shuddered. I gave her a moment while I looked over the articles again.

Minnesota. It's where I was born. How do we find each other like this? This woman and I and thousands of others who have never met but are from the Tribe of Broken Souls.

"This isn't about me. I've been healing my own way for a long time now. For a couple years I have been involved with another survivor—my partner Teri—and we've developed a loosely knit network of people across the country who take the work seriously. We do what we can to help others when regular means have been exhausted. We follow cases, court proceedings, and headlines. . Patterns. I saw this pattern that I've shown you because it's personal to me. I'm from that area and I know how the freaks operate up there. I am NOT wrong about this." She looked hard at me, waiting. I didn't doubt her. Didn't say a word.

"A very small handful of people know what we do and who we are. We use . . . unconventional methods. Off the grid, below the radar."

She smiled a little at me and went on.

"I read about you, and I read between the lines. You went the extra step against those who hurt you. We need you with us. You have the instinct. I'll fill you in on the rest, but I need to know for sure that when all else fails, when law enforcement and even family members have given up, when the courts fall short because their hands are tied, are you willing to go further?"

2

FRAN SAID THAT she would contact me later in the evening after she talked to her partner about covering my expenses. When I asked her where the money came from she hesitated for a moment, looking at me and weighing her answer. She told me then that they extorted the freaks before they took them down. I nodded and told her what I needed. The money could be left with my banker, Chris.

I had a couple hours to kill and decided to tie up some loose ends in Uptown. Chris dropped me off and smiled his knowing smile as I got out at Loretta's house in a neighborhood of old money and fine wine. I had met Loretta Provenzano at the Café Du Monde. She zeroed in on me like a gator on chum. I was what she was looking for, she told me one day as we sat near each other on the patio. By intuition, she knew that I had almost no sexual experience. Outside of a couple clumsy moments when I was 14 and again at 15, I was practically a virgin. My bio-father spoke of sex and women like garbage. It was so low on my radar that I had to be reminded that I had natural urges. Loretta reminded me. A lot. She was 33 years old and knew exactly what she wanted. I had no idea. Her recent mission was to find my dominant self by having me tie her up. I don't like having a person helpless before me, but it turned her on, so it turned me on. I spent the next hour and a half tying up her loose ends.

When I woke up at 6 and crawled out from under Loretta's out-flung leg and arm, I quietly dressed, stepped out to the parkway into stifling humidity and hopped on the St. Charles trolley. I hopped off at Canal Street and called Chris to pick me up. I sat on a low wall and sweated and smoked for about 45 minutes until an urban ghost car pulled up.

Chris picked me up in a cream colored two door '76 Cutlass Supreme with a black vinyl hardtop. It had seen better days. In the few years that we've known each other, I had never seen him in anything but his cab.

I walked around the rusted hulk, making a big show of checking it out. Chris was hanging out the driver's side window, watching me with one eyebrow raised. I pointed to a piece of the bumper that was hanging off and started to say "Hey, you know this . . ."

"Shut the fuck up, man. I'm serious."

He tried to mean mug me, but gave it up because he knew that I don't scare.

"I'm just sayin' . . ."

"Dude! Seriously, get in the damn car. Your bug-out bag is in the trunk."

Fran texted Chris when I was getting in and said that her partner agreed and came up with ten grand for my expenses. Finally, enough money to make what I do profitable. Chris just shook his head.

"You know I'm gonna have to drive you up there, right? You don't have enough ID to get a library card. Never make it past security and you can't fly for cash anymore. You gotta have plastic for that."

I didn't say it, but I was grateful that he stepped up for me. He's my banker so he's already in for ten points and we didn't discuss it, but I decided he was going to get 30% more to make it a 60/40 split. I began thinking of him as my big brother, but I'd never tell him that. I wouldn't hear the end of it.

I TOLD CHRIS that I was going to see my father and he aimed the corroded Cutlass west on I-10 for the 25-minute drive that took us to the bayou boat slip north of La Place. I didn't like being up before noon and was in no mood for Chris's bubbly humor and he knew it. He spared me and we made the trip in silence until he dropped me off at a boat slip on the north end of town and said that he'd be back for me in a couple hours.

The weathered, toothless guy in the marina office was passed out drunk. His head was pitched back over the back of his wooden office chair and flies flew in and out of his mouth, alternately landing on his gums and tongue. I left a fifty on his desk, walked down the dock, stepped down into a belly boat with a five horse Aquabug motor, and slid into the steaming bayou on a course for Esteen's cabin.

I don't like the bayou and nothing that lives there likes me. Except my father. I don't like bugs, and there are some there that aren't in any biology book. Every snake I motored by was poisonous and the gators never showed themselves completely but showed me their eyes and splashed their tails to let me know they were there and waiting. I remembered little of my four years in Minnesota, but I still had flashes of forest and clear cool lakes. I dwelt on those as I looked for the landmarks that led me to the cabin that was still a ways off.

I saw my father sitting on the deck as I cut the engine and drifted up to the dock. Since Miss Jovetta died, Esteen moved back to the swamps and had no communication with the outside world. If someone needed him, they could come to him. He took her death hard. His once short brush-cut silver hair had grown to his collar like a silver mane and he had become ill tempered. But his mind was intact. His gun metal gray eyes pierced as intensely as ever.

He was sitting in the ornate antique wheelchair that we left behind when he lifted Miss Jovetta into the canoe to take her to the "Big House" years earlier. The foot paddles were tucked in and the wheels had been locked. It had become his deck chair. It had ornate handles with a raised carving of a gator wrapped in a snake on each and I still marveled at the craftsmanship as I walked up and sat in an old lawn chair beside him.

"Palaver?"

"Yes, Sir."

"Okay. Let's smoke first."

He stepped into the cabin, came back in a moment with two black coffees, and set them on top of the crawfish trap he had flipped up on end as a table between the chairs. He took out the makings and deftly rolled a cigarette in the time that it took me to reach in my pocket, shake a Marlboro out of the pack, and light it.

We smoked in silence and listened to the morning sounds, watched the swamp things move in and out of the shadows of the stunted cypress. We saw a Macaw with a flame-orange chest and fire engine red wings land silently in the highest tree.

"Must have been someone's pet."

"Oui."

After a while I went in the cabin, refilled our coffees and we smoked in silence again. I had been there for thirty minutes before he turned to me and said, "What ails you? You have to leave and play in the darkness some more, oui?"

ESTEEN WANTS ME to have a brighter simpler life, but I just can't see that happening. I'm young, but I don't see a future of me as a citizen.

I laid out everything I'd discussed with Fran. He sat silently, smoking and drinking coffee. His eyes never left mine and he listened intently. He had always given me his full attention and likewise, as he was teaching me about life, I regarded him with the same attention.

"This network. They are vigilantes. Like you. Why do they need you? What can you do that they haven't already tried?"

Vigilante? Me? In the movies, that was my favorite character to root for, and in the comic books, guys with no superpowers like The Green Arrow got my attention. But I knew danger in real life, and down in the dark places there are no heroes, only survivors. I survived the worst shit, and I have been helping others, for a price, to survive too. Or win. That's more accurate. I want the good guys to win, even if that means that the bad guy has to die. Win or die, that's what I broke it down to subconsciously. Vigilantes always seemed to be on some mission of street justice. I don't see it as a mission. More like a necessity. Good guys? Not me. Not many of the people I helped. We're just the better ones. The one's who don't steal innocence. Vigilante. Huh.

"Fran said she read about me, but Liam Nation made sure that my name or picture never made it to the paper after that first high-profile thing we were involved in."

My father pondered this for a minute and said, "Mayhaps it was one of those internet blogger types who dug deep enough, or maybe somebody on the force who is connected to the underground and reports important news to the network you mentioned."

Maybe. It didn't feel right, but that's why I came to him. He helped me see outside of the box. Like the question of what I could do that they weren't already doing. We talked some more, and he caught me up on what Sophie was up to. She was the Medical Examiner for her parish and had some interesting cases come along now and then. But more importantly, he said that she had a man in her life."

"Do we like him?"

"Not sure, 'cher. I've met him. We'll see. We'll see."

I made it back to the boat slip and smoked until Chris showed up. I was early and took the time to think. Sophie spent hours with me teaching me how to center myself, to find the calm inside that was required to see my way through a thing. Before I could go where I wanted to in my head, I had to be in the moment. I turned my face to the humidity filtered sun and listened to the activity on the dock, smelled the fetid bayou and the Cypress that provided the canopy. Within a couple minutes I opened up to the degree that I could hear a palmetto bug clicking along a dock plank and the plaintive whines of a litter of puppies somewhere nearby.

I replayed every word that passed between me and Fran. I analyzed the gut feelings that I had about each topic that came along. No one wrote about me. There was no article, which told me that the story they said they read about me was bullshit. I knew that for sure as I sat there. I needed to know exactly why they came to me. But I was paid, and that would buy me time to get more answers. I didn't come up with much else by the time Chris rolled up, but I was calm inside for the first time in weeks. I was about to wade back into the darkness, and I was mentally locked and loaded.

3

BOOKS AND MOVIES were my school as a kid, and in the last couple years I took it upon myself to dive into history and literature. I discovered a great interest in American history. So, as Chris pointed the rusted Cutlass donkey cart North, I smoked and stared out the window. I knew that the whole route to Minnesota was formerly part of the Louisiana Purchase, and that legions of Spanish, French ,and the native Indians had covered the same ground. It meant something to me that a few hundred years later the likes of me would be a part of that fraternity of travelers, trappers, warriors, riverboat captains, murderers, thieves, and gamblers.

We stopped in Memphis for a thirty-minute break and hit the road again. Even at 2 a.m., the humidity was so thick you could chew the air. Hours later the sun rose through a filter of thick haze. We had breakfast at the In the Toolies Truck Stop in northern Iowa. The restaurant, convenience store, and gift shop were in front and the trucker's lounge with showers and a media/game room and a bank of phones was in the back.

This truck stop was a place I had been to twice before. Each time the weather was bad and I found myself drinking coffee and spending the waitress' shift with them. That's all it took to have a melancholy moment. Coming back to this Truck Stop was like returning to an old neighborhood. Before I was a Robineux, I was a 16-year-old kid that spent nearly a year hitchhiking around the country, on the road for the deed I had done to my bio-father, and never stopping anywhere for more than a few weeks. I had spent my entire childhood moving around the country in an RV and it was in me to keep moving. In the Toolies held all those wandering memories for me. I recognized both of the waitresses—the young farm fresh cute one, and the tall rode hard and put away wet cougar with a two-inch scar that started under her eye and went over her cheek bone. We sat in her section. I knew from late nights talking to her years back that she was one of us.

We ordered breakfast and I took the time to go over the files that were now on my friend's cell phone. I read them twice and when I finished I had more questions than answers. Chris called Fran to let her know that we were just a couple hours out of Minneapolis, and she gave him an address in a section of the city called Dinky Town. The address was Jim's Donut Shop, and somebody would meet us there if we called when we were twenty minutes out.

I took the job because this network was doing what I do, only on an organized scale. I've never seen an organization operate, not enough life experiences yet, but if everyone was on the same page like my Robineux family, then I wanted in. I knew as a kid what it was not to have anyone help. I can help now.

People who want to survive and lay low know enough not to set up meetings at bars and strip clubs. That's Hollywood. Hollywood can get you killed. Coffee shops, restaurants, and food courts work for us. These folks were definitely on the same track as I was when it came to security. The donut shop was perfect. Plate glass windows on three sides to watch the street, and booths for privacy. Hiding in the open.

I hadn't seen her in six years, but there was Theresa, my sister, stepping out of the donut shop and . . . my stomach flipped. My legs felt like liquid and I grabbed Chris' shoulder for support. I don't rattle easy, but I almost shattered apart as she stood before me, tears pouring out of her eyes and streaming down her cheeks. I didn't say anything, but I reached out for her and she stepped in, wrapped her arms around me and squeezed. Silently sobbing. There was nothing to say. When we had last seen each other I knew what she had to do, she knew what I had to do, and neither one of us expected to see the other again. Good things don't happen often to people like us. We stayed locked like that for a minute more, letting the poison out. Chris faded into the shop.

This was who Fran called Teri. We went inside and she started talking while we all drank coffee. My sister was the head of what I came to think of as The Network. After she threw away the trash I left behind in the RV, she went out on her own, traveled to Minnesota, and started hearing the whispers on the streets about kids going missing and ending up in the slave trade. She was made for the gig, same as me. Her freak radar was always up. She felt out the other members of The Tribe and let them know she was there with them and they could fight with the sort of justice that the courts were unwilling to hand out—not just for themselves, but for all of their kind, and so the Network was born. The money came from extortion. First timer freaks were extorted then taken down. They were usually good for fifteen to twenty grand. I meant to ask her what "taken down" meant when Fran came through the door.

"Teri has had two attempts on her life." Fran

pulled up a chair and joined us. She had just flown in, she said. "I was in New Orleans following up on a victim's relocation when I got a message: Teri's bed got shot up, through a window, on a night she slept on the couch after staying up late watching a movie. That was the second try. The first attempt was when her brakes got cut and bled out visibly on the street to send her a message."

She looked at me and went on, "A contact of ours in New Orleans told us about you once and after I heard about the shooting, I put out feelers for you. I snapped a picture of you while you were reading the newspaper accounts of the abductions and after I left you I sent her a report and that picture. She told me who you were then."

I nodded, but inside I was chilled. I had missed her snapping a picture. Situational awareness was part of my martial arts training from Sophie. Missing something even that small could be fatal in certain situations.

On TV and in the movies, when two long lost siblings find each other, they catch up on each other's lives and chat about family members and their kids. Theresa and I didn't do that. We talked about the present, the job we were here for, and enjoyed each other's company. Chris and Fran broke away and as they made their way to another booth, I heard her say, "So, you're the driver? That's it?"

MY SISTER TOLD me that Fran's abductors, Rod Hilde and Jimmy Tapio, were both out of prison and the women knew that the child-rapers were back in business because they read an online news report that the missing Minnesota girl, Ashley Hultgren, had been found alive in the Ontario wilderness just north of the Minnesota state line. She said she didn't know where she was kept because of blindfolds, and that she escaped immediately after they did a back room surgery on her. They didn't give her a sedative, one of the men in the room punched her unconscious and laughed while he did it. It was dark when she woke up and pulled off her blindfold. They left her a minute too long when they thought she was still out. A train's whistle woke her up and she quickly went out a window and screamed in pain when she landed. She had been stitched up and her stitches snapped. Fear and adrenalin carried her to the tracks and she jumped in an open box as the train rumbled right next to the building she came out of. It was a dark night and she didn't notice any of her surroundings besides the train that was going to rescue her.

One of her kidneys had been cut out of her. The

way we saw it, they were harvesting organs from the kids and selling them, but keeping them alive until they were used up. Ashley said one of her abductors smelled like oranges. Then Fran knew it was them because she smelled the same thing when she was abducted and molested. That stink was in her nightmares.

Fran had escaped during a blizzard that collapsed the roof of the shed that she was held in with others. She scaled the wall with two kids pushing her over, then burrowed her way through three foot drifts and 40 mile winds for a few hundred yards to the interstate. Twenty-eight below zero and she wore nothing but jeans, sneakers, a top, and a hoodie.

Hypothermia and frostbite were setting in when she reached the shoulder of the road. Within a minute a fast approaching snowplow barreled at her through the blinding snow. She leapt into waist-high snow in the ditch. Buried for a few seconds, she was able to dig out fast and stumble over a bank. She landed on her knees directly in front of a Datsun that was in an out of control slow-motion 180-degree spin. The driver did a double take at the kneeling apparition and immediately ducked behind the useless wheel, not wanting to witness the collision of steel and flesh.

He missed her by inches and came to rest 100 feet away in a snowbank. He shifted the little Datsun into reverse and rocked it back and forth until it came loose, then backed up to Fran and helped her in. She had hypothermia and one of her toes was frostbit, but she was thrilled to be free.

She testified against the two men that she had pointed out in an array of mug shots. Both had misdemeanor records. It was a big case ten years ago and made all the local press statewide. Even the cable news picked up the story for one day. Now they were out. Theresa had the attempts on her life and now Fran had to worry about Tapio and Hilde.

Both men were the sons of influential and wealthy men. Tapio's father was the grandmaster of Saint Paul's Winter Carnival and a commercial contractor worth a few million. Hilde's father owned a feed and seed chain that had locations in 6 Minnesota farming communities. The Network suspected that it was these men's connections that kept the slave ring going.

"They're not selling these kids to freaks overseas, they're keeping them here. In Fran's case, they were kept in locked stalls in a barn. A customer purchased a kid and was then given a key to that stall. We think that a similar setup is operating again, maybe at a storage unit facility or something like it. These kids are just meat for the wolves that pay a price and come to feed."

Chris and I turned down an offer from Theresa to stay at her one-bedroom place. We found a motel where Chris set up his laptop and we studied maps, T.V. and newspaper reports, people finder searches, and local sex offender registration sites. I pulled a yellow notepad from my go-bag and started taking notes about whatever tugged at a corner of my brain. We, meaning pretty much just Chris, cross-checked the names of the victims—those from both before and after Hilde and Tapio's time in prison. Chris scanned the older businessmen's LinkedIn accounts, and all the other social media profiles and newspaper archives for the freaks, the kids, their parents, officers involved. Chris saved what was important on the computer. I wrote notes.

It had been dark for hours when Chris went to his room to smoke a joint and watch Adult Swim. I smiled at his mellowness. He had been Army infantry in Bosnia and eventually a Special Forces counter-insurgency operative in Chechnya. He was living his life how he wanted now and doing fine.

I went to sleep thinking about Theresa. When I had talked to her earlier, I realized how matter of fact and hard she sounded. She sounded like me.

4

THREE OF THE most important things that I've learned in the last few years are that things are not as they seem, people lie, and life hurts. More for some than others. When I woke up and after I had a smoke and coffee, I settled into the spartan chair the motel provided, calmed my mind and started turning over what had been said, printed, implied, and photographed involving the freaks, their old victims and now the new ones, the survivors, and the Network. I looked for a thread hanging—anything I could get a hold of that was out of place.

If the Hilde and Tapio fathers and sons were back to slave trade, the kids weren't going to be found alive. The convicts had too much to lose to leave witnesses. They would keep them alive as long as they were profitable. Money from organ sales was "Go to jail for the rest of your life" good. The moneymen/clients had to know that these two were taking care to not leave survivors. That would make them accessories to murder. Everyone was in this up to their chins. The circle had to be tight. I could only see one way in; I had to go to the streets and start there. It's where sex money goes to get spent.

I stopped by Chris' room and let him know I was going into the streets.

"Don't fall in, Lightweight. Call me later, I'll see what I can come up with online."

Minneapolis was one of my stops when I was hitchhiking for a few months as a teenager. I knew that Han's Café was where the street tribe went to meet up, reboot, and discuss business. It was a safe haven for the runaways and the mentally disabled who had a hard time on the street. Female, male, and Transsexual prostitutes, dealers, short-con artists, and the nearly homeless elderly that we called the Home Guards came there for a break from life. My people.

I showed up at Han's Café on Hennipen Avenue carrying an Army Surplus Korean War rucksack, my traveling bag of choice, stuffed with clothes, beef jerky, instant coffee and loose packs of Marlboros. I found a booth in a back corner facing the door. There were 12 people in the room and, to a person, they all turned or glanced up when I came in. They didn't miss much.

Two girls, probably runaways, kept casting sideways glances at me. Across the room, a forty-something hard looking flinty eyed leather clad biker chick wore a blue bandana knotted in front like Rosy the Riveter. She stared straight at me over her coffee and looked me and my gear over. She held my eyes for a second and gave me a brief nod. Across the booth from her was a young Ojibwa girl with cute cheeks who looked my way occasionally, then looked at the woman across from her and spoke too quietly for me to hear.

I ordered coffee from the fluffy middle aged waitress with one milky eye, picked up a Minneapolis Tribune that had been on the seat and started reading. I didn't want to look like the desperate new guy in town who was craving company. I showed confidence and caution. People needed to know that I wasn't bullshit.

I hadn't finished the front page when the biker chick rolled up and sat across the booth from me. In the world outside the streets, people would be pissed off or offended if someone sat across from you without introductions, but in this joint, it was the way you introduced yourself to the new guy. It let you know whose house you were in.

"Who are you?"

"Vin."

"Vin? Like Vincent?"

"Sure. Something like that."

"I'm Gypsy. Some people call me Momma."

"Hey, Gypsy."

The Ojibwa girl rolled up and squeezed into the booth with Momma. They were both full figured, so there wasn't enough room to slide a piece of paper between them.

"I'm Lucky."

"I'm Vin."

"Like, Vinny?"

"Sure."

The three of us got up to smoke outside and as we passed my waitress, she flashed me a smile showing off a grill of five teeth. They looked like burned corn kernels. The movies glamorized the people of the streets, but reality was my waitress. She had a gig, barely, but she was street.

We all stepped out and lit up.

"You're on a mission." Momma wasn't judging me. Just telling the truth that she saw.

"I see those Red Wing hiking shoes, at least eighty bucks. Your clothes are worn but they're clean and they fit. No tattoos, smoking Marlboros instead of generic or roll your own. You're not angry and few of the guys around here are bright enough to read a Tribune. I figure you're looking for somebody."

"You see a lot, Momma."

"Hell, Lucky here saw half of it. We were scoping you out and she was listing it off. We don't miss much."

Lucky smiled at me and I saw crazy in her eyes. The kind of look that told you, if you were listening, that every day with her would be a bipolar roller-coaster ride, maddening but never boring. Gypsy invited me to go to her apartment to smoke weed and meet her Old Man. I didn't smoke weed, but I needed them to trust me, so the three of us headed three blocks up Hennipen Ave. to her third floor walk-up. Her boyfriend introduced himself with a biker handshake—an open fist in the air in an arm wrestling pose.

"Call me Six Pack." He was about forty and had the Kris Kristofferson whiskers, growl, and squint down like he had practiced it his whole life. I looked him over, checked his balance with my handshake.

"Call me Vin."

"Like Vin Number?"

"Right."

Six Pack had a bong loaded, so everyone gathered in the tiny living room and I smoked weed for the first time. I had always passed when it had been offered before, but I thought it would be a good move if I partook. It seemed ceremonial, a lot like the pipe being passed at a pow wow.

My first inhale was almost my last. I coughed so hard and so long that I thought my eyes would pop out. The other three grinned, coughed, and nodded their heads at me as if to say, "Welcome." We passed it one more time and I told them what I was up to.

I needed their help, their eyes and ears on the street would help me find a lead into people looking for kids, or maybe even a kid like Fran who got away and could tell me what they knew. Gypsy and Lucky both had a story about molestation at an early age in their lives and they understood what I was about.

"Fuckin' Chimos." Six Pack's fists were clenched. Knuckles white. Everybody was in.

Gypsy had a burner phone, so I gave her Chris' number and went down the stairs and out to Hennipen Avenue. I looked up and down the street and . . . had no plan at all. I was stoned. Coffee, I wanted that, so I went back to Han's Café. Everybody was watching me; I was sure of it. I was the center of attention to every citizen I passed, and the cop rounding the corner, and the children being pulled along all looked back at me. I didn't like being stoned.

Jonathan Tapio, Jimmy's father, was the founder and CEO of Tapio Commercial Contracting, LLC.

The night before, Chris had had tracked down the addresses for all of the men involved and had printed up a map of the company's Minneapolis corporate headquarters in the central business district downtown. I took out the map, saw that it was walking distance, and headed that direction in the long, steady concrete-eating stride that I used when sharking my way through unknown waters. I learned that a steady confident pace showed that you knew where you were going and that you were not a statistic waiting to happen. I stopped at a Greyhound Station along the way and put my gear in a bus locker so that I could move freely through the city and grab a bite to eat without drawing attention to myself. I had just been at Han's, but smart people never ate there.

Tapio's office was in a ten story steel and glass structure on Lasalle Avenue. I wanted a spot where I could watch the foot traffic in and out of the building, just to get a feel for the place and maybe see one of the faces that Chris and I had researched on the computer.

There was a sandwich board sign on the sidewalk in front of the building across the street from the office that advertised a rooftop restaurant. A glance up showed me that the restaurant was about 15 floors up and had a great view of the entrance to Tapio's building.

I went through the lobby and rode an elevator alone to the top. When I stepped out onto the 15th floor, I looked both ways to find the restaurant. At the end of the hall I caught a glimpse of Theresa, carrying what looked like a pool cue case, step through a door marked Employees Only. I started to call out but decided to follow her instead. I sprinted down the hall, caught the door, stepped in and quickly closed it behind me. We were on the roof next to the restaurant where the massive A/C unit and small electric station sat hidden behind shrubbery at the restaurant's request. My sister was kneeling by a short wall facing the street and I walked up quietly and knelt down beside her. She looked at me for a second, opened the case and pulled out a .22 long rifle.

"Why a .22?" I didn't know much about guns, but I had fired a .22 when I was a kid.

"Because it's quiet and the bullet tumbles rather than rotates, so you get maximum damage."

I reached for her chin gently and turned her to face me. For five seconds we looked into each other's eyes. She was vibrating. Her eyes were jumping and they were dilated. Her hands were rock-steady, but I could see veins in her neck and forehead throbbing in third gear.

"Is this who you are now?" It was a simple question with no judgment in it.

"I'm sending a message. If I kill both fathers, the sons will know why. The police won't know who or why, but the sons are ex-cons with connections on the street and they'll come looking. I'm pretty sure they're the ones who tried to take me out before. This time it's my turn."

"You make killing sound easy. It's not. I killed two men. One was our father, both were freaks, and I never lost a minute of sleep over them, but my soul was scarred over."

She glanced at me. "These are not the first. They're just next. There have been others. All freaks."

She was speaking out the side of her mouth while aiming at the entrance across the street. As she finished her last sentence, Tapio got out of the passenger side of a black car in front of the building and as he turned to talk to his driver Theresa exhaled slowly through her nose and shot him in the heart from about 200 yards.

I didn't try to stop her. It crossed my mind, but my heart wasn't in it. These predators needed to be put down like any other rabid animal. Theresa lived through being raped by our father, getting pregnant from it, and protecting me—her rape baby. Because of her, I was ready when it was my turn to dance with that freak.

No words or movement were wasted as she put

the gun in the case, turned, and we started for the door. I followed her to the elevators, and we caught one with two people coming out. Theresa pushed the button for Level 1 Parking. I could see she had an exit plan so I just flowed with it.

When the elevator opened, she walked up to the bed of a white pickup and reached over the side to unlock the truck box in the back. She set the rifle in the box, locked it and nodded towards a Vespa parked near the wall. She dug out the key, and I sat behind her as she fired it up. We made our way through the parking structure to the street level exit on the opposite side of the building from the shooting. A Minneapolis P.D. cruiser blocked the exit.

When we stopped, a cop got out and walked toward us. His hand rested on his 9mm but you could see the tension leave him as he approached a scooter with a female driving and a young man on the back. We didn't fit the shooter profile in his head.

"Get some helmets." He turned on his heel and walked away.

"Yes, sir."

THERESA'S APARTMENT WAS spartan like mine. Even with a thousand miles between us, we were living each other's lives. I didn't feel truly alive unless I was trying to take down a predator. Theresa tracked them and killed them.

"I wanted you to find me. I wanted you to see my work and to see if my blood would join me." She put two coffees down, sat across from me at her tiny kitchen table and lit a Marlboro Light.

It struck me sitting there that I was the incest baby of a rapist pedophile and a cold blooded vigilante killer. The Gasparilla blood line of the 21st Century having coffee and a smoke after a killing.

I sat quiet and smoked. Theresa got up and left the room, leaving me time to sort it out. I wanted these malfunctioning humans taken down but I was getting weary of the chase and because of it I was missing out on truly living. At my age, most young men were getting out of college and going after their careers, apprenticing in some construction or mechanical job, slinging rocks on a corner in between prison bits, or tramping around the country. I missed the road. The few months that I traveled around five years earlier lit a fire in me and the flame never burned out. I wanted to walk out of her apartment and just walk away from the hunt and never look back. I would have, but it felt right watching the freak get put down.

Over the last few years I found these animals for their victims, and once for the cops, but it wasn't enough. There were thousands just in the U.S. The court system failed because it wasn't the solution in the first place. Extermination worked.

Theresa needed me to flush them out so she could put them down. I could do that. But I needed to talk to sister Sophie first. Part of the martial arts training that she gave me was focused on the roots of a fighter's intentions—what was in his heart and soul. I was starting to worry about the callus on my heart.

"YOU'VE TAKEN IT to the next level, haven't you?" Sophie had a 'second sight' that ran strong and deep in the Robineux family. Her grandmother Jovetta had it as did her mother before her. She always knew when I was going through a thing.

"Yes, but not as far as you think. Someone else is doing that . . ." I told her then about running into Theresa and without going into specifics on a cell broadcast she got the whole picture through innuendo and by what wasn't said. When I finished, there was a pause of about 20 seconds and I heard my sister quietly sobbing.

"There's only one way this can end, Vin, and you know that. If you don't die, you spend most or all of your life in a six by ten box. When our father brought you to us, it felt like you were coming home, as if you had always been a part of us. There is a power in that.

We see the man you can be, and he may not show it, but father worries for you. You are still so young, and still haven't given yourself a chance to be . . . anything you want. What *do* you want in this life, Mon Cher?"

I had never been much for naval gazing. I used to dream about far-away places and fascinating people, but that flame sputtered out. Almost. For the past six years I woke up every day hoping I could take down another freak. I had the Robineuxs to keep me from going off the rails when things got dark. They kept me from becoming Theresa.

"I want to see what's over the next hill, what's around the next bend. I want to walk away from people who need me and the ones who love me and go on a walkabout. I'm sick of living in the shadows and dealing with the dark people. I don't know if I know what I want, but I know what I don't want anymore." I told Sophie that I wouldn't do anything until I took some time to think about things, and she told me that she loved me.

I wanted all that, but how could I walk away from Theresa and what she was doing? She wanted me to track them, but she could do that. I saw that earlier that day. Chris came all this way, but I had already paid him his cut. The ten grand that the Network came up with was traveling and expenses. They wouldn't be out anything. But there were a million predators and only a few warriors trying to take them out. I decided that I could do both. Freaks were everywhere that I wanted to go, I didn't have to seek them out, somehow we found each other. If I came across one, I would deal with them. But I knew that was bullshit. I couldn't walk away and leave this loose end in Minneapolis. I committed to this case before I left New Orleans, and the missing kids weren't going to live through this if I didn't find them. I had some ideas about where to start.

ALL OF THE women in my life lately were warriors, and I sat with them that night at three long candle-lit break tables deep inside a long-abandoned Greyhound bus barn that the street tribe led us to. The wooden building was about seventy-five years old and fifty feet high. On one end there was a long flight of stairs leading up to offices with a connecting balcony that encircled the interior. Gypsy, Lucky, and Six Pack ran off the handful of homeless that were living there and told them to take the message to the streets that the property was off limits for a month. They only had to explain that it was about protecting kids, and everyone being evicted nodded in unison. If the law got wind of it everyone knew that street law would leave them dead in a dumpster.

A couple hours earlier I asked Chris to put out a group text about a No Drugs or Liquor rule when we were discussing business. Everyone agreed. Theresa, Fran, Gypsy, Lucky. Me, Chris, and Six Pack all crowded the tables. Some of us smoked, and everyone had a bottle of water. Theresa, Fran, and Lucky made it clear that they thought the freaks had to be made dead. I brought up the fact that we needed to find and secure the kids before they started knocking off targets. Theresa agreed to follow behind us after we got what we needed.

We split into groups- the three warrior/killers that spoke up would be a hit team. Six Pack wanted to join them, but I told him there was money to be extorted and I needed him as a "persuader." He nodded and grinned. I'd seen that look on Dobermans before.

Chris would set up wire transfers when the time came for the marks to pay up. Gypsy and I were going to focus on the rescue. She showed me pictures on her phone of her in a cocktail dress looking plus-sized smokin' hot and another of her in cowboy boots and a Wrangler shirt and jeans on a barrel racer quarter horse kicking up dust. She was a chameleon, and she was going to be the "face" of the operation. I would stay in the shadows.

CHRIS RODE BY Clay Hilde's house in St. Paul while
I was on the roof of the office building with Theresa
earlier in the day. He told us there were security gates
and dogs and we decided it would be easier to get to
Hilde at work. He owned six Feed and Seed stores
in southern Minnesota and his business office was
in Wilmar, but when Gypsy called posing as Anne
Sathers, a commercial real estate agent, Hilde's secre-
tary said that he was rarely there but that she would
forward her number to him. The only way to catch
up would be to try to catch him at one of his other
feed stores. Chris brought up his profile on a social
media page and there was a picture of Clay Hilde in a
dark blue Dodge Ram diesel dually pickup, heavy on
the chrome and illegally dark tinted windows. That's
the truck we would be looking for at each location.

Theresa and the other women got a room in Wilmar to wait for our call when we found him. We
didn't want to spook Hilde by asking around for him,
and his other stores were in a 50-mile radius of Wilmar and easy to drive to, so we decided to try to catch
him coming or going. Chris drove his abomination;
Six Pack rode shotgun and they went to Clara City. I
rode with Gypsy in a rental car that Chris picked up
on a credit card and we drove toward Spicer.

I needed Six Pack to sit with Hilde in a room and
pick his brain about where the kids were being kept,

and to persuade him without mercy. If we found him, we would meet Six somewhere so he could do his thing. I would do it myself, but I wanted to be the hole card in the game. No sense in letting them know our numbers. We were bringing a war to them, and we weren't sure of their numbers. Besides the fathers and sons, there were any number of possibly dangerous customers involved in the child rape network.

As we drove toward Spicer, Gypsy and I worked out the details of our plan. I called Sophie and let her know what I had decided. She sounded relieved and I needed that. Her, Esteen, and Miss Jovetta before she died, were my anchors. I decided after calling her, that after all of this was over, I was going to look into my heritage. I knew that my bio-father was from Minnesota and I was already here. I would look into the Gasparilla family and see just what stock I came from.

We had been on the road for about a half-hour when Gypsy got a call, listened for a moment and handed me the cell.

"Hey, this is Lucky. We must have been followed. That Fran chick is dead, strangled, and your sister is M.I.A."

5

THE WOMEN HAD just checked into a room at a roadside motel when Fran got a call, stepped out of the room and out of sight. Theresa got up about ten minutes later and stepped out without saying a word to Lucky. Ten more minutes and Lucky knew things had gone bad. She saw Fran's empty car in front of the room and walked around the side of the building into an alley. In her experience, dead people end up in dumpsters.

Fran's body was in an industrial dumpster that the motel was using for remodeling scrap. Lucky had to reach up and stand on tip-toes to see the woman she had just met, sprawled out with her arms and one leg spread at angles only the dead can achieve. One leg had been left dangling over the edge. The killer wanted her found.

She had been strangled with a strip of bed sheet

that had been left around her neck, and Lucky said that she would never forget the image of Fran's swollen purple tongue protruding between her blue lips. And that the body smelled like oranges.

Lucky got excited when she told the story, I could see it in her eyes. She was a special kind of psychopath.

". . . and I don't know where your sister went. She left her cell phone back in the room."

"What did you do with the body?" Our tribe didn't call police. It was the same wherever I went.

"Tossed her leg back over the edge, threw some scrap on her and left her there. Then I went back to the room and got a hand towel and wiped down everything we touched in the room and the dumpster and scrap that I touched." She'll do.

Strangulation is close-up work and not for everyone. It's one of the ways convicts take care of business on the inside. Young Tapio or Hilde must have caught wind of our crew, the word was out on the street after all, and followed us. Theresa left ten minutes before Lucky did, she must have found Fran and might have even seen the killer. She was in the wind without a phone and I couldn't do anything about it.

I called Chris and had just filled him in on what was happening when Gypsy pointed out the big Dodge truck in front of the Hilde's Feed store. The business was attached to an old grain depot and silo along the tracks that ran along the length of the town. There was a big red Ford truck next to the blue one and there were three boxcars on the track behind the building. There was a loose thread there, but I couldn't get ahold of it.

We parked two blocks away at a second-hand store and Gypsy went in. I waited in the car and listened to a BBC report about female genital mutilation in an African country. I started to go cold inside. It was a different kind of freak that needed to control women and force them to damage themselves for life, but a predator is a predator. There really were not enough hunters in the world.

Gypsy came out of the store with her long brown hair combed out straight and looking full-figured-farm-girl-sexy, wearing a plaid shirt with pearl snaps and wrangler jeans that were well worn.

I stepped out of the car and into a blue-collar bar next door to the thrift store to wait while she drove to the feed store. She needed to be by herself in order to lure him out.

I bought a Budweiser, took a couple pulls off the bottle, and realized that I didn't have a cell phone or anyone's number. Fuck. I was pretty sure Theresa could handle herself, but there was no good reason that she hadn't tried to reach out to anyone yet and no way for her to reach out to me. It struck me at that moment what a Luddite was. I was going to have to get a 21st Century device if any of this was ever going to work.

We figured it would take Gypsy just fifteen minutes to do her thing and it turned out to be almost 30 minutes before she came in the back door of the bar, caught my eye, and turned around and walked out. Her hair was tussled and I thought I saw blood on her lip.

I followed her out and we both got into the rental car and hit the road, leaving town while Gypsy called the others to let them know where to meet us. Hilde was trussed up in the back seat, zip-ties around his wrists and ankles and a rag stuck in his mouth. I looked a question at her and she just said, "Chloroform. He fought harder than most. He was noisy waking up so I stuck a rag in him." She was definitely a force to be reckoned with.

The box cars behind the feed store had A/C units on them. They had to be for produce or people, and these guys didn't sell produce. It hit me hard.

"We have to go back!"

The big red Ford that was at the feed store slammed hard into the rear of the car just as the words came out of my mouth. It knocked the rear out to the right and Gypsy over corrected to the left over the center line causing the car to spin into a 180 degree turn, but the spin was interrupted when the big-rig cattle hauler hit the passenger side and spun us into the oncoming truck that rammed us. The last thing I saw before my window exploded was the Ford emblem on the grill.

Part II

Theresa

6

CALVIN WAS AIR lifted to Hennipen County Medical Center and lived another week in the ICU. The right half of his head was caved in, the right eye and ear ground up in the crash. He lost his right arm at the shoulder, and both legs were still hanging on him but were just meat sacks of splintered bone. His liver and spleen and one lung were lacerated by a piece of metal that drove through the back seat and through him. He was in a full body brace, but they didn't bother casting him. Nothing was reparable.

Esteen had been contacted and I met the steel eyed Cajun and his stormy eyed daughter when Esteen and Sophie's flight landed at 3 a.m. on the night of the day Vin was hit, and they had been here every day with the rest of us. They called him Vin, but I grew up with Calvin. Being dug in with the Robineuxs in a hospital for two weeks was rubbing off on me and even I started thinking of my brother as Vin. The short version did fit him.

Gypsy made it through just fine with a broken wrist, huge bruises, and a ragged slash in her thigh that needed stitches. She waited in the lobby with Lucky and Six. They were there every day for hours.

Chris took his turns on night watch at Vin's bedside. On the night of his first watch he shared all the information he had researched with Esteen, and after the two men had spent hours together and parted ways, Vin's closest friend and brother went ice cold when anyone tried to talk to him. He wouldn't talk to anyone or respond to a question. I could see the wheels turning behind his eyes and I knew that he was very much in the moment around Vin, but he was looking right through everyone else. I figured he was going to come apart.

MY SON REGAINED consciousness after a couple days. His brain, jaw, and voice box were still intact and slowly, between morphine naps, he told us what happened. I kept trying to get him to rest, but he wanted to tell us more in case we could use any of it.

He lost consciousness again and didn't come back to us until two days later—the day he died. Sophie and Esteen were in the room when he faded to black.

They said his whole body, or what was left of it, seized up. He coughed up black blood and died with a long wheeze.

Calvin was cremated two days later. Esteen walked out of the mortuary with his ashes and no one tried to stop him. Chris left right behind him and we never saw him again.

The child rapers killed my son, my brother, and my Fran—the only woman who ever loved me. They fucked up. I was going to go Viking all over them.

THE COUNTY SHERIFF said that it was a hit and run homicide, and they were on the lookout for a big Red Ford. Old Man Hilde wasn't in the car when first responders arrived. I didn't mention to the cops that we might have figured out where the missing kids were. The system had been failing all along, no need to involve them now. We would do what needed to be done.

That night Six Pack, Lucky, Gypsy, Sophie and me were in the same motel room that Lucky and I stayed in a couple weeks earlier. We wanted them to find us.

Sophie and I had been sizing each other up ever since she arrived. I wanted to like her, but there was a way about her that pissed me off. She was completely confident and centered. I've met only a couple women like that in my life and she was the kind of woman I wanted to be. Attractive in a clean-scrubbed athletic way but she had a smokey sexiness that didn't need make-up. I wanted her even now—so shortly after Fran's death, but she was Vin's "sister" and that was enough for me. I knew that she had trained my son to fight and that went a long way with me. She knew who I was to Vin and I could tell that she gave me credit where it was due. We understood each other.

ESTEEN WAS IN the wind, but Sophie said that she "felt" him nearby and that he wouldn't hesitate to kill. I believed her. He didn't know the players, so I figured that if he was the guy I thought he was, he was in the dark covering our door and all the access points. He was 70 years old, but moved like a man of 50. I don't like many people and almost no men. I liked him.

Vin had mentioned that he saw A/C units on top of the box cars and figured they were for keeping the kids alive. The rest of us were betting on it. No one knew exactly how many kids there were, but we figured that more than six would be too many to manage and keep alive, so Gypsy and Lucky left to find a passenger van to steal and planned to ride over to the box cars to break the locks and load kids. Gypsy said that on the day she lured Hilde out that there was only a teen farm kid working the counter, so they didn't expect any problems they couldn't handle. They would take the kids to a family restaurant down the road, send them in to call 911, and drive away. If any of them needed medical attention right away they would drop them at the little hospital on the edge of town. None of us wanted to talk to police.

Sophie worked side by side with the law in her job as a Medical Examiner, but justice and the law don't always agree, and when it came to family, she chose justice without hesitation. She really was a piece of work. She knew I was a shooter and she immediately stepped in beside me in planning even though she had warned our brother about doing the same thing.

Chris had tracked all the players' addresses and texted that information to us all a couple weeks earlier. Jimmy Tapio lived in Hastings, about 150 miles east of our motel in Wilmar.

Six left for about ten minutes and came back with a nondescript white Taurus. When we loaded up, I pointed out that the steering column was still intact. He nodded. "Yeah. Had the keys in it. I had my pick of three cars in that lot with keys. Small town folks. Too easy."

Six Pack came along because, "I gotta make some

Short Eyes bleed." When I mentioned that Jimmy Tapio was one of our targets, Pack's head came up slowly and his eyes narrowed.

"I was in Stillwater with that freak. I met him because we were getting stitched up in the infirmary on the same day. He was in PC with the rest of the molesters, but one of the Aryans stuck him six times. Caught him when he was gettin' his hair cut.

"I got nailed in the head with a mop ringer on the cell block and had to get 14 stitches. Tapio was getting two stitches for every puncture. He cried like a bitch . . . dude smelled like oranges. Still can't get that stink out of my head."

Fucking oranges.

Tapio killed Fran. Like his father before him, I was going to erase him.

7

GYPSY CALLED WHEN we were on the road and told us Lucky killed a big redneck posted on watch on a fold-up chair near the first train car. The guy was napping when the psycho-warrior bitch rolled up behind him and garroted him. He stood and lifted her off the ground, but she held on and almost severed his head before he fell dead with her riding him to the floor. Fucking garroted him. Gypsy was tough, but she was still seriously creeped out from hearing Lucky's sensual moaning as she took the guy out.

There were five kids in the box cars. Zach Karpinen and Ashley Hultgren were malnourished, glassy-eyed, and both showed the women that they had had a kidney removed. There were two 13-year-old girls that were snatched from Ontario, one just stared off into nothing when the women tried to talk to her. The other was a shaking terrified mess. They had been marketed and sexually traumatized as a pair. Corey Maki lay in a corner unconscious, and looked like he had taken a beating more than once. The women unloaded all of the kids at the ER entrance at the little hospital. They put the Maki boy in a wheelchair and had one of the kids push him in. The warrior women got into the wind then and waited for us to call when we were clear.

WE STOPPED AT a 24-hour drugstore in Hastings as soon as we rolled in. Sophie came out with a box of surgical gloves and shoe covers that went on like slippers over our shoes and we all put them on. We got to Jimmie Tapio's neighborhood at midnight. He lived in a modest split-level ranch style home that backed up to a park. We parked on the far side of the park and jogged in a low crouch through the trees and twice out into the open because we had no choice. It was a moonless Tuesday night, so not much chance of being seen at that hour.

Once again, we relied on Chris's earlier research. He had mapped the house with a satellite app and saw where the security camera placements were. We all were sent a link and had studied it days earlier.

I hunkered down behind a knee-high rock and assumed a firing position. Six Pack and Sophie crouched behind me. I had outfitted my .22 with a night scope and had a new suppressor on it; even though the crack of a .22 bullet is quiet, I wanted to be careful. I took out all three cameras that covered the back of the house in three shots, shot out the security lights next, and we moved in.

The lights were on in the kitchen and we could see through the patio door that a flat-screen was on in the living room. It was the only thing left standing. All of the furniture, the sound system, and bookcases were tipped over and most of them smeared with blood. As we carefully walked in with all of our senses tuned in to sights and sounds, we could see Jimmie Tapio's head, arms, and legs sticking out of the middle of a glass coffee table. There was a bloody aluminum baseball bat on the floor next to the coffee table.

Both of his arms were shattered at the elbow, and both of his kneecaps had been pulverized to the point that each one bled freely and saturated his khakis. Every bone in his face had been broken to the degree that the skin looked like it was just a sack holding in gravel. His cheeks were caved in and his jaw had been ripped open and hung useless on his chest. His mouth was filled with shards of broken DVDs, probably child porn films, and his lips were shredded to confetti as the jagged edges were shoved in. He was definitely awake when that happened. It made me smile.

There was a Yellow Cab key chain stuck in one eye. The short chain dangled from the eye socket.

Chris.

He took my kill, but Vin and Chris were brothers, so . . . fuck, I really wanted to be the one to make that freak die.

8

Esteen

OVER THE PAST century, the Robineux family had become a tribe rather than a bloodline. Jovetta, an only child, never had children. She was sixty years old when she took in Esteen Gasparilla, the son of Rusk, her lifelong friend and protector, and raised him as her own.

Esteen was nine years old when his fourteen-year-old brother Thomas exploded the top of their father's head with a shotgun in his sleep. Thomas wasn't being abused, he just wanted to see what killing felt like. Esteen never saw him again. His mother, a former prostitute in the glory days of Storyville, had died from complications of his birth, so he was totally alone. Jovetta didn't wait a full day before she moved the boy into the old Antebellum home with her.

Esteen struggled with what he subconsciously called Beast. The old Cajun did three tours in Vietnam. They tried to send him home after two, but he re-upped. When there was killing to be done, Beast consumed him. He had hunted Camille's killer for years, and Beast raged with fury when the man who murdered his wife went to his home when Esteen wasn't there and Sophie had to kill the man. Miss Jovetta died shortly after, and her death kicked the air out of the old warrior. He had retreated from the world and Beast rumbled quietly in its cage until the freaks killed his son.

SOPHIE HAD TEXTED him three hours earlier when they found young Tapio. He didn't respond. In his mind, there was nothing to say. Hilde had a cabin in the north woods on the shore of Lake Vermillion, and that's where Esteen was now. He had parked his rental in a marina parking lot, and made his way through acres of white birch forest behind a line of cabins. Internet maps had shown him that the address was the fourth cabin from the marina. About a half mile.

By now both father and son Hilde had heard about the Tapios and the kids, and the cabin seemed like the next logical place. Prey often hides in places that are familiar to them. Hunters know that.

The veteran fighter didn't bring a gun. They would die by his knife, a twelve-inch long Arkansas toothpick made of Damascus steel. He would do it for Vin, and for the children and all civilized folks. He wanted the ex-con first. It was his blue Ford that killed Vin. Esteen wanted to cut his heart out and feed it to the corpse. He saw it in his mind as he waited.

He set up in a four-foot wide and three-foot deep gap between two twenty- foot moss covered boulders of granite that were near the sparsely forested shore and downwind of the cabin. Downwind meant he could smoke and eat the fistful of Slim Jims that he brought for the recon. It could be a long wait. The sun set and it quickly became a dark moonless night.

FORTY-FIVE MINUTES later, Ron Hilde fantailed dirt around the hairpin turns on the winding backwoods road leading to the cabin, barely missing trees and dislodging large rocks in his big dually Ford. He skidded to a stop by the porch, jumped out and opened the rear door of the crew cab, reached in with both hands, pulled his father out by his collar and let him drop to the gravel drive in front of the cabin.

Clay Hilde was still trussed up with the zip ties that Gypsy had put on, but instead of the rag she stuffed in his mouth, his son had replaced it with duct tape. He had road rash along one temple and well into his hairline. One eye was black, and his shoes were missing.

"You're about a dumb motherfucker, old man. Kept the kids right next to the store?! You know how hard it was to get those little squealers?" Ron kicked his father in the face and broke the man's nose. Blood flew and Clay Hilde's eyes bulged from lack of oxygen. His mouth covered and nose broken had left him no way to breath. He started grinding his face in the dirt, trying to dislodge the tape from his mouth. One corner loosened and he gasped for a breath as Ron's work boot caught him in the jaw, right below the ear, and he blacked out.

"Don't you fuckin' dare pass out! You fucked it all up!" Ron kneeled down and slapped the older man's face so hard that it sounded like a small caliber gun shot. Blood flew from Clay's destroyed nose, then he pissed himself, but he was still out.

Ron tried to stand up but there was a burning pain in the back of his neck and his legs wouldn't work. He looked down and saw the four inches of blade that was sticking out of his neck, right above the collarbone to the right of his esophagus and he saw the blood pouring down the front of his shirt. The shock dropped him to his knees.

Beast raged.

9

GYPSY AND LUCKY met up with Theresa, Sophie, and Six Pack at a truck-stop in St. Cloud. They found a corner booth in the restaurant and Theresa handed the Minneapolis street tribe each an envelope of cash. Two grand apiece.

Six Pack shook his head and started, "Man, I didn't even get my hands on any of 'em . . ."

Theresa was talking to them, but looking at Sophie when she said, "You all stepped up and stood up when you needed to. I know we'll see each other again. There's only two freaks left, and they're the reason our brother is dead. We'll take it from here." Sophie nodded and allowed a thin grin. They both lost a brother. The line between Robineux and Gasparilla was blurring. The two clans had merged.

Gypsy let the warrior sisters know, "When it comes to kids, hit us up anytime." The Tribe got into the van that the two women had stolen earlier to re-trieve the kids and drove away.

CLAY HILDE CRAWLED away from a bloody horror. It was night and there was blood in his swollen eyes and at first it looked like a sinewy, tanned old wolf was cutting into Ron Hilde's chest with an enormous hunting knife. Not a wolf, maybe, but it was snarling that woke him up. And growling. There was blood everywhere, and in the dark it looked like black oil.

His feet were still bound and he had to roll quiet-ly away. He almost yelled out in pain twice when his broken face grazed the earth. He got his hand on a sharp flat rock and took a couple seconds to cut the bindings off his feet, but he didn't have time to work on the zip-ties on his wrists.

He got up and ran then. Not into the cabin, which had been in his family for three generations and was well stocked with guns, but into the deep pine and birch forest that surrounded Lake Vermillion. He didn't need a gun. He had survived days in those woods as a boy during the family's summer visits.

He was about the same age as the psycho that he saw slaughtering his son, and nearly as fit. Clay Hil-de was a hard, grizzled farmer become businessman. Never one to stay in one place long, he spent his days moving from one feed store to the other, moving stock around, working side by side with his employees when a customer's truck need to be loaded, or an incoming freight car needed to be unloaded. He hunted, fished, and hiked for a week at a time. He was strong and he was a sociopath—he had fucked the corpses of a mother and daughter that he had killed when he was 15. He had forced mentally handicapped elderly men and women to give him head when he worked in nursing homes to pay his way through college to get a degree in Business Management. He wasn't raised by cruel or deviant parents; he was just born bad.

When Ron came to him about snatching kids years earlier, he saw right away that there was money to be made off of what he had been doing to Ron since he was 7 years old. Clay Hilde liked to defile kids because it was taboo in every culture in the world. He like the power of robbing innocence. It wasn't about kids really—it was about the wrongness of it. He embraced the idea of breaking kids' spirits while making money off of the other freaks that he knew. And then the wheels came off.

Beast was coming, Hilde heard the brush of denim on a rock or tree. His senses were amplified by becoming the prey. The darkness in the forest was thick on a moonless night and he depended on his sense of smell and hearing. Who the hell *were* these people?

10

Sophie

A GATOR WRAPPED up by a water moccasin is a symbol, a sort of family crest, that is inlaid into the bow of a canoe that rests in the rafters of my father's shack in the bayou, and the same symbol was crafted into the silver handholds on Memaw Jovetta's antique wheelchair.

Growing up, I came to believe that the image represented danger—a warning of the things that are teaming up to get you. I never pondered it further, but Memaw spoke to me about it one lazy afternoon on the back boardwalk-style porch behind the old Antebellum bayou house.

"Mon Cher, you know that your daddy was born a Gasparilla?"

"Yes Ma'am, he told me a couple years ago. He said that his great grandfather murdered your great grandfather, and that your Grandfather-Lucient killed my daddy's Grandfather-Antoine."

"Oui, there was a feud of sorts over generations. The mothers of the two families never had a say in the course of events until now. That ended when Esteen's daddy died, and he became my son."

"I never married his father, Rusk Gasparilla, but he was the only man I ever truly loved. I never had children but he had twins from a working girl in an underground bordello that he spent one drunken night with. She died at childbirth, no-one knew her real name or anything about her, and Rusk took his offspring home.

"Robineux and Gasparilla, bound to each other and equally as dangerous. I am the end of the family bloodline, but you and my son are the Robineux legacy. I saw this in a vision and I made the symbol that I was shown. The Gator and Snake are the two families."

I THOUGHT OF that conversation as Theresa and I rolled down the rutted road to Hilde's cabin. It was dark and there were no lights on in the cabin when we rolled up. Theresa killed the lights and turned off the ignition and we both just sat silent a minute, listening for whatever. But there was nothing to hear. Rod Hilde's truck was there but it was empty. Nothing stirred. Anywhere.

We found the dead predator behind his truck. I had heard about my father's rage from Memaw, but seeing it illuminated by a cellphone flashlight made my knees go liquid. I grabbed Theresa's shoulder for support and I could feel her vibrating.

I tried to assess the situation professionally, noting that my father had hobbled the victim by cutting the tendons behind his knees and inside the elbows. He had stabbed him through the neck rather than up under the rib cage where he would have hit an organ and caused death almost instantly. He wanted the killer of his son to be alive when he opened his chest and removed his heart. The half-eaten heart lay in a pool of blood and mud a couple feet from the body.

Our clan was eliminating the fathers and sons of deviant marauding clans even now in the 21st century. I had killed a man years earlier that Vin and Esteen had been hunting for the death of Camille, my mother. We all had blood on our hands, but we were the Good Guys, right?

I looked at Theresa and thought about what Vin told me about her sniping Tapio from the roof of a building, and that she said it wasn't her first kill. I looked down at Ron Hilde and the bloody hole in his chest and the pool of blood, made black by the night. Good Guys, yes. If not us, who? The Law had its chance. Who else was stepping up?

I had spent my childhood in the bayou and surrounding countryside with my father as a guide and teacher, I knew wilderness, so I led us out into the Northern Minnesota summer night as we tracked one of our own.

11

Vern

VERN HAUTILLA WAS a 38-year-old combat veteran from the war in Bosnia. He was a trapper, hunter, fisherman, a lifelong bachelor and a natural fit for his job in the Minnesota Department of Natural Resources Law Enforcement Division. The Commander that he was assigned to in the Vermillion Division, Bruce Barden, was an old classmate he had hunted with many times, so about six months into Vern's service, Barden turned to him, the best tracker he knew, to track a four-year-old child who had walked away from his family's camp in the middle of the night, probably to pee, and had disappeared. The boy had been missing for two days and a search party of 34 people weren't able to find him. It took Vern less than five hours to find the little boy.

No-one had bothered to look up during the search, but Vern had tracked him to a grove of trees and the tracks disappeared without a sign of a scuffle. Vern saw where the boy's shoe had scraped bark from the side of a Balsam Fir, and when Vern looked up he saw the boy nestled into a cluster of branches, fast asleep. He had been on the job for three years and had never had a day that he hated.

He was smoking a Marlboro and picking fat blueberries from a patch next to his state issued truck at sunrise when he heard a roar and saw two impossibly bloody men crash through a patch of chokecherry bushes and roll down a slope into the gravel road across from him. Neither one of the combatants moved at first.

Vern's brain went on automatic. He radioed in his position, called for an ambulance that he knew would be at least thirty minutes away out of the nearby town of Orr, and when he was told that back-up was forty-five minutes out, he immediately took control of the scene.

One of the men rolled halfway over towards the other one, grabbed a bloody spearhead shaped rock and began to lift it when Vern drew his department approved personal sidearm and said firmly and loudly, "Don't!"

Clay Hilde froze. He looked up to see a .45 revolver aimed at him in a steady hand.

Vern had never drawn his weapon on the job before. DNR Law Enforcement doesn't usually encounter much more than an occasional angry response from a hunter or fisherman receiving a citation and the very rare legendary backwoods meth lab, so their weapons may never be drawn during their entire career.

When Vern had been involved in firefights in Bosnia, he had a semi-auto side arm that he never drew. He had only killed with his M-16 and once he had killed three Serbs in a bunker with a shoulder mounted L.A.W., but now, staring over the barrel of his.45 Colt revolver, he knew that he would do the right thing in this civilian job. He was calm and prepared to pull the trigger. Esteen turned his head and coughed a bloody foam.

HILDE HAD FASHIONED a spear during the night and had risen out of the waters of a swamp as Esteen crept by on the shore and had driven the stick through Esteen's chest before the Cajun's Arkansas toothpick caught the freak just above the hipbone and drove into his intestines, but missed any vital organs. Esteen fell to his knees, his blade slipped from his hand into the swampy shoreline and Clay Hilde slipped away into the dark water. Moments later, the wounded Cajun heard the predator crawl up the shore across the swamp.

They hid from each other but Esteen stayed on Clay's trail at a distance. They both spent much of the night field dressing their wounds with what was available. Esteen knew that he had a punctured lung and that he could live through it, but he couldn't lose consciousness, not until he killed Hilde. He would have to get ahead of him at some point for an ambush. He didn't have the wind for a knuckle and skull fight. And his knife was gone.

When Esteen finally leapt from cover, it was just turning sunrise. He moved fast with a spearhead shaped rock that he had fashioned overnight. He drove it into the same wound above Hilde's hip. Hilde roared and Beast growled.

They wrapped up in a death struggle that found them lying in the road. Esteen saw that the guy with the gun saved him from getting his head smashed in, then the world turned to black.

VERN HAUTILLA HANDCUFFED Clay Hilde and let him lie where he was. The man was loosing blood from what appeared to be a knife wound. Vern went to the truck quickly and returned with a large gauze pad and tape from his first aid kit and field dressed the wound as best he could.

Esteen was unconscious and not going anywhere, but Vern trussed him up with zip-ties from the truck because he had seen what these two had done to each other. He carefully searched both men, expecting to find a knife, but came up empty. He stood and took a long moment to just look at the men. It looked like it had been an epic battle.

Sophie and Theresa stepped into the clearing a couple minutes after he had secured his suspects. They both saw the men on the ground, could see the rise and fall of Esteen's labored breathing and knew that he was alive.

Vern saw Sophie first but his heart leapt into his throat when he saw Theresa. Her chestnut hair was wild, she had just a slash for mouth and her pink flushed cheeks were topped by blazing sky-blue eyes. She walked with the confident upright carriage of a fighter and with the rippling rolling shoulders of a big cat. There were no soft edges to her; her slight breasts and lithe body seemed to vibrate slightly with kinetic energy.

Both women stepped on each other's sentences demanding to know why Esteen was cuffed and de- manded to know just who this other man was and what was going on. Vern ignored their questions and asked them why they happened to be in this remote part of the woods.

Sophie told him a story about how her and her father had flown to Minneapolis to have a reunion with her cousin Theresa, and a three-day fishing trip to Vermillion was on Esteen's itinerary before they returned to New Orleans. They got concerned when he hadn't called in in two days and they decided to come to the section of State Park that he had marked for them on a map.

"We weren't sure that anything was wrong at all, but we thought we might come up and surprise him if we found him and just camp with him on the last night. But then we found a trail of blood and some strips of bloody bandages and knew that my father needed us."

Esteen came-to when he heard his daughter's voice but he didn't open his eyes, he heard her story then passed out again.

Vern never took his eyes off of Theresa the whole time Sophie was talking and when she finished he said, "Bullshit."

"Bullshit?" both women said at once.

"You betcha, bullshit. Nothing you just said explains one thing about what happened here between those two men." Vern was still looking at Theresa when he spoke. She looked amused.

Sophie stepped between the other two so that he would be forced to look at her. "Look, Mr. Ranger, we just got here, that's my father laying there, don't be an insensitive douche."

12

Clans

SOPHIE AND THERESA sat at the Northwoods Café, just one block from where Esteen was resting after having been stabilized in the ICU of the Laurentian Medical Center in Virginia, Minnesota. The two women had been just a few steps away from Esteen's bedside for 48 hours and they were still weary and emotionally fried from holding vigil recently with Vin, so both agreed that they needed to get out of there for an hour.

Sophie Robineux, Medical Examiner of Boudreaux Parish, knew how to talk to Law Enforcement and Assistant District Attorneys, and over two breakfast burritos made with that special Minnesota brand of bland, she laid out to Theresa what she learned in the two days since Esteen and Clay Hilde had been airlifted out of the Vermillion State Park.

"Vern says it's a waiting game until Daddy wakes up to tell his side of the story. Hilde clammed up and is waiting for his lawyer to drive up from Minneapolis. I spent the morning using my credentials and waiting for them to call Louisiana about my bona fides and then time on the phone with the ADA explaining that this was just a reunion gone horribly wrong and that my father is the victim of a savage unprovoked attack by a stranger."

"Did they buy it?"

"Maybe."

Sophie pointed. "He wants you."

"You told him I'm a Lez?"

Sophie nodded, "Yeah. He said it doesn't matter to him. He just smiled."

"Jesus, that's pathetic."

Sophie took a drink of the beige warm water that passed for hot black coffee in that joint and said, "So, I have to get this off my chest since this is our first sit down together with no-one else around; Esteen Robineux was Esteen Gasparilla before Miss Jovetta legally adopted him. His brother was Thomas." She let that sink in while she winced through another drink of the brown water.

Theresa stayed silent for a few moments then

leaned in a little, her elbows on the table, and whispered loudly, "Fuck!"

She stayed in that position for a moment more, getting more pissed off as another dynamic of the situation hit her from a different angle as she thought about how much she was attracted to Sophie so soon after Fran's death. She sighed out another whisper, "And fuck again."

"Did you know that Thomas killed their father Rusk and when Esteen asked him why he did it he said he just wanted to know what it felt like to kill?"

Theresa shook her head, stared out the window at the hospital across the street and said, "And Calvin, Vin, whatever, killed our father Thomas. Gasparillas kill. It's who we are."

"I've killed a man too," Sophie said, "And I am a Robineux, as is Esteen. Miss Jovetta made sure of that. Sometimes your family gets to pick you. Vin was Robineux too."

"Bullshit. That's all hoodoo bullshit. Besides Calvin and Fran, no-one picked me."

Sophie grinned, and Theresa leaned in again and said in a low growl through her teeth, "Fuck you for grinning. The fuck is wrong with you?"

Sophie closed the gap, leaned all the way in until the tips of their noses were touching and said, "You chose us. Don't you see? There's no reason for you to be here with me right now. Vin's killer is locked up, the abducted children that survived are safe, and the rest of the bad guys are dead. *We* are your family. You sat with me at my father's bedside and here we are now, Cousin, together. It's in the soul, not the DNA. Robineux and Gasparilla have become one."

13

Vern

VERN HAUTILLA STARTED at the point on the road where the two men had landed after they crashed through the tree line. He wasn't expecting much after so many First Responders had tracked through the scene, but he started there with the intention of working backward until he was satisfied that he had the whole picture of how the conflict started.

He knelt and picked up the rock that Hilde attempted to use. He stayed on his haunches and turned the tapered rock around in his hand. He could see the man-made chipping and flaking that had been done to it, giving it a spear shape and fashioned into a fine weapon. He admired the work, bagged the rock and tucked it into a day pack that he had taken with him from the truck.

He was a tracker and he was in his element. His heart rate slowed, his senses were clear and alert. A scuff on a rock, berries knocked from a bush, broken young limbs each told him something about how things developed.

The trail was easy at first, both men battling and crashing through the undergrowth for the last fifty yards before they came out in the clearing, but as Vern followed the sign, it became more of a challenge. Both Hilde and Esteen were obviously skilled woodsmen. They had both been careful of not stepping on dry leaves or twigs, walking on large rocks whenever possible. He found a spot where one of the men had knelt, bled, and covered the spot with pine needles. At another spot he found a swath of blood smeared where someone had leaned on the flaked paper-like bark of a White Birch but didn't bother or have the time to hide it.

Vern found the spot by the edge of the swamp where Hilde had whittled a spear, and he saw mashed down weeds under the surface of the swamp where the man had crouched in wait for the other man. Both men had lost blood, it was everywhere. Vern knew by Hilde's wounds that Esteen must have had a knife, although he wasn't carrying it when Vern encountered them, and he knew that this was most likely the spot where he would have lost it in the dark.

The Ranger knelt, searched with his hands through the water and silt for a few feet along the shoreline and found the Arkansas toothpick. He let out a small "Damn," at the razor sharpness and craftsmanship of the blade. The handle was bone with a scrimshaw design of a gator wrapped in a snake. He bagged it and put it into his pack.

Both the farmer and the old Cajun had lost a considerable amount of blood and had been going on straight grit and stamina. The tracker quickly gained a respect for both men's survival instincts and skills as he followed their signs. He found where Esteen had hidden and waited.

For who? He looked at the cabin. It looked deserted and there were no vehicles parked in the dirt drive in front. He walked up to the nearest window, cupped his hands and looked inside. There was dust on the kerosene lamp inside on the windowsill and there was a spider web running from the windowsill to a nearby overstuffed chair. No one had been there for a long time.

Vern stepped off the porch onto the driveway and crouched for a close look. Someone had raked out tire tracks and had scattered hands full of leaves, pine needles and detritus from around the clearing all along the drive to the first curve.

He walked around the area in concentric circles

until he found where what should have been packed earth had been removed to a three-inch depth in a ten square foot area then replaced with loose dirt and covered with the same materials that were everywhere. He was crouched down, resting on his haunches, and he could smell the blood.

He saw a glint of yellow hanging from the lowest limb of a small balsam fir a few feet away. He didn't reach for it right away, just pondered its existence for a while. Because of where it was hung, it was obviously left for someone checking signs. After a couple moments he removed the little yellow taxi, keychain, bagged it and started to put it in his pack, but for reasons that were a mystery even to him, he put it in his pocket instead.